Lost at Sea

Linda Bello-Ruiz
Award-winning author

LOST AT SEA

By award-winning author

Linda Bello-Ruiz

www.mariahpublishing.com

Lost at Sea
First edition
© 2019 by Linda Bello-Ruiz
All rights reserved.

This is a work of fiction, inspired by actual events. Names of people and places have been changed to protect privacy.

ISBN: 978-0-9895258-7-9
Published by Mariah Publishing, California
www.mariahpublishing.com

Cover design by Yoko Matsuoka
Typography by Yoko Matsuoka
Book design by Jo-Anne Rosen
Back cover author photograph by Ric Ewing
Editing by Jan Arzooman

Printed in the United States of America

❧ DEDICATION ❧

To all the families who have suffered the tragic,
unexplained loss of a loved one. And to you who
prayed for, searched for, and/or donated toward
the effort to find "Alejandro."

❧ ACKNOWLEDGMENTS ❧

It takes a village to complete challenging tasks, and that is especially true when writing a book. Writing is a solitary task, so having a village of friends is priceless.

Thank you goes to the Faith Writers of Lincoln Hills—Jan, Jeri, and Dory—for reading each chapter and offering valuable suggestions and edits along the way. Thanks also goes to my students at The Country Writers group in Santa Rosa and to my teachers and writing friends at the Santa Rosa Junior College's Creative Writing and Fiction Writing classes. I especially want to thank songwriter and friend Jim Wilder for lending me his expertise.

Jan Arzooman, your eye to detail and knowledge of conceptual editing has always impressed me, and you again polished this story, for which I am grateful.

I would also like to acknowledge "Alejandro's" family and thank them for their transparency and willingness to share their heart-wrenching experience and memories, which I added to mine. I pray I did them justice within the words of this book.

❧ AUTHOR'S NOTE ❧

This work of fiction, inspired by actual events, is another in the "Rebecca in La Perlita" series.

It is true that a young man went fishing in June 2017 and didn't return. And that friends, family, and later the authorities searched for him without success. Over the following weeks and months, seven theories surfaced to explain the young man's disappearance.

This book delves into those theories as Rebecca sets out to discover what happened. While those familiar with the events that are the basis for this book will recognize people, places, and facts—the author asks you to keep in mind that not everything in the story you are about to read is, nor could be, true. Names, places and details have been changed. The author used her creative license to make this book an interesting read—while maintaining privacy and staying true to the underlying tragedy.

You may have your own theory of what happened that day. The question remains: Was it a murder, an accident, or neither—is he alive?

❧ PREFACE ❧

June 2017
La Perlita, Jalisco, México

The young man bent over the side of the small fishing vessel, cupped saltwater in his light brown hands, and splashed his face. Each passing hour diminished his faith. How much longer until they return? Although he'd tried a hundred times before, he attempted once more to start the engine. Nothing. Not even a sputter.

Alejandro Garcia was adrift in a 24-foot blue-and-white fiberglass fishing boat known as a *panga*. Earlier that afternoon, the motor had failed.

The boat captain, Martin, had used Alejandro's cell phone to call for assistance and, soon after, help arrived.

"We're going to follow the fishing line to the far side," Alejandro's boss said. "We'll get the fish and return. It won't be more than a couple of hours."

Alejandro glanced around the *panga*. No life vest. No shade. No VHF radio to call the port captain or other boats. "I want to come with you." He took a step into the boat.

"No," Martin said, and shoved him backward.

Alejandro caught his balance and glared at the captain. "Why me?"

"You have a cell phone. Use it to communicate to shore if you need to. Now, do as you're told."

Lalo, ten years older than Alejandro, scratched his beard, adjusted his ragged fishing cap, stepped past Alejandro into the waiting *panga*, and stayed silent.

Alejandro plopped onto the fiberglass bench and crossed his arms.

Hours passed. The *panga* had been situated near a three-mile-long fishing line with its hundreds of fishhooks and a crudely fashioned anchor tied to a buoy. Waves had untethered the *panga* from the anchor and Alejandro could no longer see the buoy or his end of the line.

The winds picked up. Rough waves raised and dropped the boat, sending Alejandro crashing into the sides. He hung on as another large wave hammered the vessel. Regaining his balance a few moments later, he looked at his cell phone and then searched the horizon.

"Damn!" Alejandro kicked the bench. "Where are they? Martin said a couple of hours."

A scary thought hit him as he steadied himself through the rolling of another swell. Long-line fishing is illegal. Did a navy patrol stop them?

Finding an old piece of material stuffed under the bench, Alejandro fashioned a makeshift shade area at the bow. He created height by tying a long piece of fishing line to the front center of the fabric and attaching it to the top of a makeshift wooden pole the captain had secured on the *panga's* deck. He then tied the sides of the material to the mooring cleats on each side of the boat.

Grateful for a respite from the punishing afternoon sun, Alejandro put his three-inch pocketknife safely away, laid down under the shade, and retrieved the cell phone from his pocket to text his girlfriend.

Hola, amor. They haven't returned.
What's takn so long?
IDK
Where r u?
20°57'24.2N, 10°527'49.5W
Is that your location?
Sí

Waves lifted the small boat again and set it back down with a jolt. Alejandro grabbed hold of the nearby bench. He tasted the salt spray, and spit. Breathing deeply, he worked the kinks out of his neck. Just as he started to send another text, the phone battery died. *"Ay caramba!"* he screamed.

Crawling out from under the sun shelter, Alejandro again searched the horizon and fought his rising fear.

Hours later, Alejandro watched the sky. The sun began to set. A storm was brewing. The large piece of material meant to protect him from the sun now caught the wind and moved him briskly through the waves. The *panga* had turned into a sailboat.

He had to keep believing Captain Martin would return, or that other fishermen would see him on their way back into port. He caressed the round silver locket hanging on a simple chain around his neck and struggled to keep his mind focused on good things. On his family. On his young son.

Darkness enveloped him. The wind ripped straight offshore, driving him farther out into the Pacific.

PART I

❧ ONE ❦

November 2017

My plane lands at the Puerto Vallarta airport. Unbuckling the seat belt, I gather my personal items, run a pick through my hair, and wait to disembark along with a hundred other passengers escaping the cold of the north.

I am almost home.

My name is Rebecca. And even though my green eyes, red hair, and freckles scream "*gringa*" to the world, my heart definitely sings lively Mariachi songs. I have been wintering in La Perlita, a small fishing village off the Pacific Coast of Mexico, since my early retirement, eleven years ago.

The humidity hits me like opening the door of a sauna. Feeling the full force of the steam, I scamper across the hot, black tarmac. Having made this trip many times before, I am somewhat prepared. In the cramped airplane's bathroom, I have already changed my winter clothes for white capris, a short-sleeve green blouse, and sandals. Even so, the heat is suffocating, and my skin already feels sticky.

Pulling my packed-to-the-brim carry-on, I hurry into the air-conditioned immigration oasis. Relief. Arriving in Puerto Vallarta or anywhere along the tropical Mexican coast before mid-December is not for wimps.

This particular trip back to paradise is stained with a sad mission. My young friend and neighbor, Alejandro, went missing at sea in June. Five months later, there's no sign of him. I'm still in disbelief. His sister, Perla, asked me to help them find her younger brother. From my computer in California, using Facebook, I alerted the public, asked for prayers and monetary donations, and kept everybody apprised of the search and rescue effort—spearheaded by my good friend Salvador in La Perlita—the "boots on the ground."

"Next," an official calls from the customs counter. He waves me forward.

I hand over my tourist card and passport. *"Buenas tardes, Señor."*

"Buenas tardes, Señora," he replies with a smile that reaches his dark-brown eyes. *"Bienvenida."*

And with his welcome, and stamped documents allowing me to be in Mexico for a maximum of six months, I proceed to the baggage claim.

A text from my niece, Lisa, dings on my phone, advising me she's outside waiting.

Although I profess to be a retired bilingual counselor and prefer to enjoy retirement sipping margaritas on the beach—I've turned investigator. And, for the record, I've already been informed there are certain people in La Perlita who do not want Alejandro's disappearance investigated.

❧ TWO ❧

Settling in, I gaze out the car window as we begin the forty-minute drive south on Highway 200 toward La Perlita. We pass through blocks of commercial buildings, luxury hotels, and gated communities before the Puerto Vallarta Marina comes into view. Two majestic cruise ships are docked right along the road, framed by palm trees and red bougainvillea. I catch glimpses of the Pacific Ocean hidden behind high-rise condominiums. City life has never appealed to me and I'm glad I chose to live in a fishing village.

I find myself exhaling deeply every few minutes.

"Hey, Auntie," Lisa says, straightening her glasses, which always seem to slide down the bridge of her nose. "You're using up the oxygen with all that hard breathing."

I laugh. "Sorry. It's automatic. I'm releasing the strain of the north to prepare for a much calmer few months."

"That's how it usually is, but since you're all fired up to know what happened to Alejandro, how much serenity and calm do you expect this season?"

"That's a good question. I hope to get answers within a couple of weeks. And then spend the rest of the time chilling."

"You're never one to chill much anywhere," she says.

"Well, yeah, that's kinda true. But I do try."

Lisa glances at me with a worried look. "How do you think Alejandro disappeared?"

I take another deep breath. "At first I thought it was 'a tragic accident at sea,' like Alejandro's friend José told me on the phone. Now I'm not so sure."

"Why?"

"If it was just an accident, Salvador wouldn't have gotten an anonymous call telling him to back off the search."

"Did he really?" The concern on Lisa's face matches what I'm feeling inside. "That sounds dangerous."

"I agree. Salvador gave up his personal and business life for nearly a month to concentrate on finding Alejandro. To be warned off can't be good."

Lisa and I spend a lot of time together in La Perlita—a village of five thousand inhabitants that swells to seven thousand during the winter. She first came to La Perlita at age eight with her mother, my older sister. Lisa is now in her mid-fifties and manages her mom's small hotel. I can't fathom how she got that old, since I haven't aged.

My sister, Tina, her husband, and her children discovered La Perlita while on vacation in 1966. Tina brought me with her a few years later. We all fell in love with the town, the beach, and the villagers, which is why we visited frequently over the years.

Tina spent the last thirty-five years of her life full-time in the village and loved every day of it until cancer took her life a year ago. Her death leaves an empty space in my heart. La Perlita is not the same without her.

"Mom really liked Alejandro," Lisa says as the ocean comes into view on our right. "He was her favorite waiter at the *Paraiso* Restaurant. He treated her like a princess, opening her car door when she arrived, escorting her to the table, and always remembering she wanted white wine with her meal."

"And an ashtray," I say and smile, remembering his attentiveness. I exhale again—this time my released stress is mingled with sadness. "Alejandro is a special young man, which makes this so tragic. Only twenty-two, father of a toddler, and missing."

Lisa nods in agreement. She takes a rubber band from the console and captures her long, highlighted brown hair into a ponytail. "I talked to Salvador last week, right after I got into town," she says. "I went in for brochures on his bike and kayak rentals to share with our guests at the Bungalows."

Palm trees, banana orchards, and coconut groves come into view on our left as we leave the city behind. "You have people already? Isn't it early?"

"A little. Just one of the five rooms is occupied right now...an older couple from Canada. The other four are full come December first."

"Your mom would be happy you're keeping the Bungalows open. I'm proud of you."

"She worked too hard to establish herself in La Perlita for me to just let it go. But anyway, as I was saying, I saw Salvador and he asked when you would be here."

"I'll call him. He's definitely on my list as I attempt to unravel the Alejandro mystery."

Lisa drops me off at my house to unpack, with a promise to meet later for dinner. I notice the red bougainvillea blooming on the street side of my courtyard privacy wall. With a smile—glad to be home—I unlock the patio door and roll in two heavy suitcases jam-packed with summer clothes and a sundry of items for the house and yard.

The swimming pool sparkles—clear and inviting. The grass has been cut to precision by the gardener. Pink, red and yellow flowers explode from the colorful terracotta planters. Plentiful multi-color bougainvillea decorate the inside of the ten-foot wall, scattered amongst ferns and palms. After eleven years, my house and yard are just like I want them—my own personal haven.

My smile widens as I unlock the downstairs door, enter my bedroom, and then wander upstairs, turning on the numerous overhead fans. Elva, my housekeeper, has the two-story house in perfect condition—every window washed, tile floors scrubbed, and beds freshly made.

Unpacked an hour later, and after a quick dip in the pool, I pick up the house phone next to my bed and dial Salvador.

"*Bueno.*"

"*Hola.* I've arrived. Are you up for a visit this week?"

"It's about time you got back into town. Yes. Let's see. Today is Monday. I'll be in Puerto Vallarta for the next two days. Can you come by my shop on Thursday? After I close at six?"

"That'll be perfect. I want to settle in and get acclimated. This humidity makes my hair frizz. I imagine I'll spend a few hours a day in the pool or splayed out under a fan."

Salvador laughs, and in my mind's eye, I see his dimples and smiling brown eyes. "If you think *this* is hot you don't want to be here July through October."

"That's exactly why I'm not here July through October. Hey, have you seen Alejandro's mom lately?" I ask. "Is she okay...or as okay as she can be?"

"She's not good. She wanders around the neighborhood like a zombie. Hardly talks to anybody. It's depressing. She's lost a lot of weight."

"Oh, geez. Poor Rosy. How devastating. Alejandro is her baby. He's younger than my youngest by two years. I can't imagine losing a child. And to not know where he is after five months? It's heartbreaking. The pain and anxiety would drive me *loca* for sure."

I pause a moment and then ask, "Did she go back to using drugs?"

"Not that I know of. She's been clean for over a year. Given the devastation of losing a child, it wouldn't surprise me if she did relapse, though," he said.

We spend a few more moments chatting about Rosy, village news, and friends. "Hey, I'm off to enjoy the sunset with Lisa. I'll be by Thursday. I think I'll stop in and meet the port captain tomorrow. I want to hear what he has to say about Alejandro."

"So you're going to ignore the warning I received...to stop looking further into Alejandro's disappearance?"

"I know this may be naïve, Salvador, but you received the warning, not me. So, in reality, I've never been told to stay away. And I have too many questions just to let this be. But I'll be careful."

"Well, I'm not sure if the port captain is a good guy or not," he says. "Alejandro's family thinks he's corrupt, but he did help me identify the last known whereabouts using the GPS coordinates. Watch what you ask until you're sure he's on our side."

Perspiration drips down the back of my neck and I turn the overhead fan to high. "I received several text messages during the initial search from people here questioning the port captain. So, yes, I'll be cautious."

That evening, I start a list of people to interview, writing them down in a spiral notebook: port captain, assistant port captain, Salvador, José (Alejandro's co-worker), Cesar (Alejandro's older brother), Rosy, Sergio (the president of the sports-fishing association), Captain Martin and the fishermen who were with him when Alejandro was left behind (Lalo, Alfonso and Beto.)

⊱ THREE ⊰

On Tuesday morning, I ride my bike to the Port Captaincy office, five minutes away. With all my years in La Perlita, I've never had reason to meet the port captain or his staff.

"*Buenos dias*, Rebecca," neighbors call out as I pass by. "Welcome home."

"*Gracias*," I respond, keeping both hands on the warm handlebars to maneuver over the numerous speed bumps.

My heart soars with gratitude as I pedal on, feeling a light wind in my face—blessed to live the winter months in this small fishing community. Armando waves from behind the counter of his hardware store, Mariana gives me a thumbs-up as I approach her taco stand, and her eighty-year-old granny, Olga, smiles her toothless grin. The aroma of sizzling onions, chorizo, and chili peppers caresses my senses as I return the greetings with a big smile and pass on by.

Within minutes, I glide into the driveway of the captain's office and engage the bike's kickstand. Opening a heavy glass door, I peer inside. "Hello?" I say to an empty waiting room.

A short, stout man with bushy eyebrows appears from the doorway of a back room. "May I help you?"

"*Sí.* My name is Rebecca. Are you the port captain?"

"No, I'm his assistant, Francisco. How can I help you?"

I notice kind, dark-brown eyes behind wire-rimmed glasses. He is dressed in blue linen trousers and a matching blue short-sleeved collared shirt. The assistant port captain is on my list of people to interview, but not yet. "Is the captain in?"

"*Sí.* Do you have an appointment?"

"No. Do I need one?"

"Usually. Let me check if he has time to see you. What is this about?"

"Alejandro Garcia's disappearance last June."

Francisco stares at me with a furrowed brow. His kind eyes now hold big question marks. I imagine his thoughts: "What is this gringa doing here asking about Alejandro's disappearance?"

I stay silent and smile, ignoring the question marks, and take a seat in a white plastic chair.

Francisco and his questioning eyes disappear down a hallway. A few moments later a tall, distinguished-looking man with a dark mustache approaches, with Francisco close behind.

"I am *Capitán* Ricardo Manuel Vargas Torres," the man says with a deep voice. His black hair and beard, dusted with silver, tell me he's in my age group. Good looking for a senior-citizen type. I wonder if he's single, but then remember he may be the enemy. I refocus and stand to shake his hand.

"*Me llamo Rebecca. Mucho gusto, Capitán.* Alejandro Garcia is my friend. If you have a few moments, I'd like to talk to you about his disappearance."

"Yes, of course. Francisco, bring a cup of coffee for Miss Rebecca to my office, please. You drink coffee, yes?"

"*Si. Gracias.*"

"And one for me. Bring cream and sugar also, please."

I admire the captain's formal naval attire as I follow him to his office. He is dressed in starched white pants, white shoes, and a tailored white short-sleeved shirt adorned with colorful emblems above the front pockets and shoulders, which I'm sure stand for something impressive. Requesting coffee is a good sign. He is willing to talk to me and he must not be in a hurry.

"I've heard about you," he says, which surprises me.

"Really?"

"Yes. You're the Canadian who works with the town council and organizes fundraisers for La Perlita and people in need."

"That sounds like me," I respond and smile, "except I'm from the States...California, to be exact." His knowing something about me is heartening and means I won't have to spend time explaining who I am before launching into my questions.

"Alejandro is both a friend and neighbor," I explain, accepting his invitation to sit. "I've known him for years. We would often run into each other at the athletic field... me, taking a morning stroll, and he, exercising his dog. His brother Cesar is also a friend.

"I have questions about what transpired last June and hope you can help enlighten me. I'd like to understand how this office organized and implemented the search and rescue. And I'm curious as to your official opinion of his possible whereabouts."

"Francisco, make that coffee extra strong," Captain Ricardo yells down the hallway, before turning to me. His dark brown eyes light up and the corners crinkle with the full force of his smile. "Those are complex questions, Miss Rebecca. I think I need caffeine before we get started."

His teasing response makes me laugh. I settle in to pick his official brain.

While waiting for the coffee to brew, Captain Ricardo provides me a synopsis of his scope of influence and responsibility in our fishing village. He has heard about me and I, too, have heard about him. A few friends say he's honest, doing his job, while others believe he's corrupt and can be bought to look the other way on infractions. I'm here to judge for myself.

"I'm responsible for the safety of the boating community in and around La Perlita," he explains. "That means two hundred and seventy-five vessels, from expensive sport fishing boats to small pangas, which are managed by seven fishing co-ops.

"The owners of all foreign vessels, like yachts and sailboats coming into port during the tourist season, must come to this office and register on their arrival and notify us before their departure."

"What exactly is your responsibility for those who work within your jurisdiction year-round?" I ask.

Captain Ricardo spends five minutes reciting a long list of official duties seemingly memorized from a policy manual. I hurry to jot them down in my notebook.

Francisco appears with a tray holding two cups of steaming coffee and condiments, which breaks up the captain's monologue.

"*Gracias*, Francisco," I say, accepting the coffee, feeling the heat pass through the ceramic cup into the palms of my hands. The job description I've heard so far only adds to my list of questions. Inspecting boats coming in and out of port is under his command. If they are inspected, how was Captain Martin able to take out a *panga* with no safety equipment onboard?

Captain Ricardo stirs sugar and cream into his coffee while continuing his discourse. "And finally, I investigate infractions of laws that regulate maritime activities, and impose the respective sanctions."

I review my notes. "So, let me see if I understand this. You enforce laws related to sea vessels and give out fines to those who break them. Boat owners and captains must pass a test on boating safety and you verify the results. You inspect boats coming and going from La Perlita. You check foreign vessels in and out of the port. You arbitrate worker and employer disputes. And you investigate accidents. Is that right?"

"Yes."

"You have a lot on your plate. Who do you work for?"

"The Mexican Armada."

"That's the equivalent to the navy, right?"

He nods.

There is silence in the room for a few moments as we both savor our coffee. My mind is not silent, however. "So, you inspect all vessels?"

"I have the *right* to do that," he counters. "I don't have the manpower to do it regularly, though. Here at the Port Captaincy, it's just me, Francisco, and a part-time secretary."

"So, nobody inspected Captain Martin's *panga* that fateful day?"

"Nope. Not that I know of."

I'm not yet sure if I've come to a safe place, but I have so many questions to ask. "Can we talk about the specifics of Alejandro's disappearance?"

"Sure. What kind of information are you looking for?"

I take a moment to study the port captain sitting across the mahogany desk in a big, comfy-looking leather chair that fits his large frame. There are nautical charts on the wall behind him and a VHF radio on top of a filing cabinet, which I assume he uses to communicate with boats under his purview. "When did you first hear Alejandro was missing?"

"Monday evening. But it was late and a storm was brewing. We couldn't do anything."

"So, he went out fishing before sunrise on Monday morning and you were notified later that evening? Do you know what happened before you were notified?"

"According to the captain, they left to fish about three in the morning. The boat stalled mid-afternoon. Martin used Alejandro's phone to call for help and then he and another fisherman went with those in the rescue boat to collect the fish from the long-line. Alejandro stayed behind."

The port captain stares into his coffee cup for a moment and then looks up at me. "Long-line fishing is illegal, by the way."

"Isn't that when the fishermen lay out a fishing line several miles long, with buoys at both ends?"

He nods in agreement. "And underneath the top line is a second line with hundreds of weighted fishing hooks. They leave the contraption in place and come back hours later to collect the fish."

"And this is illegal?"

"Sí. Which is why Martin and his crew, including Alejandro, left under the cover of darkness. Before anybody was down at the docks. It's illegal because over-fishing by a few creates an unfair advantage over sport fishermen and other commercial fishermen who need fish for their own livelihoods."

I nod my head, agreeing with this summation. "What does the boat captain say happened, and why did it take so long to tell you they couldn't find Alejandro?"

"You do have a lot of questions, Miss Rebecca," he says with a slight smile. "He reported that when the motor failed, they were at one end of the long-line. As I said, Alejandro remained behind, tending the disabled *panga*. When they got back to where they're sure they left Alejandro, he and the vessel were gone. They searched for several hours until it got too dark to continue...and then the storm hit."

I stare at the captain for a few moments, willing myself to stay calm. "They couldn't have radioed in to you or others what was happening?"

"They didn't have a radio and didn't want to take the time to go to shore. Martin says they thought they would find him."

"And that's why it took so long for you to be notified?"

He sits up straight and his voice becomes somber. "Yes. That was unfortunate. I filed the missing person report first thing Tuesday morning."

I had heard this same story from Salvador and Alejandro's family, and it made me angry each time. Captain Martin's decision to leave Alejandro, who had absolutely no fishing or boating experience, was, to me, more than unfortunate. It was criminal.

"All that happened on Monday," I say. "I'm told Captain Martin and others apparently searched Tuesday and Wednesday. Alejandro's sister, Perla, contacted me on Thursday. The family was desperate for more people to go out looking and asked for my help to get the word out on social media. Had you also activated a search?"

"There was some confusion," he admits. "It was first reported he went missing in waters off the coast of Nayarit, which took it out of my jurisdiction. The State of Nayarit has its own naval authority."

I want to scream. That confusion over jurisdiction wasted valuable time. Even though the border with the state of Nayarit is only ten minutes away by boat, the nearest government offices are an hour away by land. Alejandro's family doesn't own a car, and they didn't want to waste daylight search hours sitting in an office filling out paperwork.

"They were frantic when they couldn't get anybody to jump in and help," I say. "And I had no idea how to proceed from so far away."

"Where were you at the time?" he asks.

"At home in California," I say. "Feeling angry and powerless."

The captain places his cup on the desk. "There are protocols. A missing person's report must be filed and authority established. I got officially involved in the search on Tuesday afternoon when the missing person's report was completed and delivered by Alejandro's sister."

I want to bounce out of my chair and accuse Captain Ricardo of not doing his job from the get-go, but I figure he'll kick me out of his office. The damage has been done and my righteous indignation isn't going to change that. So, I change the subject. "You say one of your responsibilities is making sure boat owners have passed a test on boating safety. Do you certify them with a license or permit?"

"Yes. All boat owners have the license, but not all boat

captains, as they should. Some owners allow captains who are not licensed to rent their boats."

"Well, I'm sure you've heard, from Alejandro's family and Salvador, that Captain Martin didn't have any legal fishing documents, nor was there safety equipment on board. None. The only GPS was Alejandro's cell phone."

I feel tension seep into the small room as my voice takes on heat.

Captain Ricardo attempts a tired, woeful expression and then stands, causing me to sit back in my chair and wonder if he's had enough of my questions.

Instead, he comes around his desk and sits on the edge just inches from me. He places his hands in his lap and with restraint in his voice says, "*Sí*, and I have sanctioned the owner and filed an extensive complaint against Captain Martin for a long list of infractions."

His response gives me pause. Okay, so maybe he is one of the good guys and did his job, but I still have questions. Before I can proceed, however, Francisco opens the office door. "Your eleven o'clock appointment is here, Sir, and you have two phone calls on hold."

"*Gracias*, Francisco. I'll be right there. Thank you, Miss Rebecca, for your visit today. What is your ultimate goal, by the way? Are you curious, or are you filing an investigative report?"

I smile a bit to ease the tension and take a deep breath. "I want to make sense of what happened to Alejandro. And I don't want this to happen to anyone else. Ever. And, I have hope that Alejandro is still out there."

"Why?" he asks.

"Because no boat, body, or any item from the boat ever washed ashore. That's why."

Captain Ricardo lowers his voice. "You know, another boat went missing that Monday night. A big, fancy, well-equipped fishing boat, with two young men onboard… one an experienced, licensed boat captain. They drove right into the storm. They didn't return either."

"Yes, I know. Their families contacted me on Facebook while I was reaching out for help in finding Alejandro. But I understand their case is different and Salvador counseled me not to get involved."

He escorts me to his office door. "Salvador counseled you well. Even though I had raised the red flag to shut down the port that night, those young men took off anyway. I'm pretty sure they were gas runners for the cartel—and had been ordered to take fuel to a passing drug boat out in the Pacific."

"That is its own heartbreaking story. But, Captain Ricardo, I believe Alejandro had nothing to do with drugs or any mafia-type group. He was a good kid. And he's missing. I have more questions. May I come to see you again?"

He reaches out to shake my hand. "That's fine. Make an appointment. And go easy on me next time. Okay?"

His wry sense of humor broadens my smile, and I laugh. "I'm sorry if I sound like an interrogator. I'm frustrated with this whole situation and want answers. It's been five months tomorrow. Alejandro took that job to earn money for a baptism party for his young son. It's heart-breaking."

He nods in agreement and I walk down the hall to the reception area.

Before leaving, I pop my head into Francisco's office and wait a moment for him to finish a phone call. "May I help you?" he asks.

"I'd like an appointment on Friday to see the captain, around ten o'clock. Is he available?"

He looks down at the appointment book. "He has an eleven o'clock slot. Would that work?"

"Sure. And Francisco, what do you think happened to Alejandro?"

Francisco doesn't hesitate. "Did you see the picture Alejandro sent to his girlfriend via text before his cell phone died?"

"The one that showed him near a large white rock out in the ocean?"

"No, the one that shows he used a large piece of cloth to give himself shade."

"I remember seeing that on an internet news report," I say.

"Well, I believe the cloth, tied down to the sides of the *panga*, became like a sail on a sailboat, and when the winds picked up that afternoon and evening, he was blown way off course—which is why he wasn't found where the last cell GPS coordinates placed him."

I digest that theory for a moment. "That makes sense. But on day four, after being delayed by bad weather on Thursday, a seaplane was up and searching for him. And a friend of mine sent out a private plane from Mexico City. The seaplane explored up and down the Nayarit and Jalisco coast and the larger plane searched out into the Pacific. Neither found any evidence of Alejandro."

I stop for a few seconds to settle my rising sadness. "If the boat overturned in the high waves or crashed against a rock, wouldn't it, or Alejandro, eventually have washed ashore somewhere? Or would the *panga* just have sunk with Alejandro inside?"

"*Pangas* are made of fiberglass, Rebecca. They are long, narrow and canoe-shaped, with a high bow that provides buoyancy. There's a flotation bulge on the top edge of the hull. Simply put, they are specifically designed to stay afloat."

"So where's the boat? Where's Alejandro?"

"*No lo sé*. We all wonder the same thing. I also knew Alejandro and his family. I personally joined in the search."

I see sadness in Francisco's eyes and get the sense he's another one of the good guys. I thank him and return outside to my bike. Before I can place my notebook and purse into the front basket, perspiration is dripping down the sides of my face. Eleven in the morning and it's that hot.

I've been in La Perlita for less than twenty-four hours. My head is spinning with old and new information. It's time to get into my pool and think through my next courses of action.

≈ FOUR ≈

The next morning, I awake with a start, trembling, my heart racing. Tears stream down my face. I take a deep breath and exhale. *An Alejandro dream.* Closing my eyes, I struggle for a moment to remember. The dream comes into focus and lights up in front of me. I was a seagull flying above Alejandro in the *panga.* The sun had set and the night turned cold. I watched Alejandro take down the fabric shade and huddle beneath it, shivering. I felt his desperation. *It's been two days. They'll come for me tomorrow. Please, Dios mio,* I heard him plead.

He licked his hot, dry lips. The skin had begun to crack. I longed to give him a drink of water. I wanted to hold and comfort him.

Where are they? His desperate question reached out and touched me in my core as I soared above.

A blackness billowing against the backdrop of the sunset caught my eye. A line of storm clouds was closing in on him. Closing fast! There was nothing he could do about it. There was nothing I could do.

Leaving my bed, I open the curtains of the French doors and gaze outside, full of grief despite the dawn of a new day. *Alejandro, where are you? What happened that day?*

Tentacles of the dream stay with me. Was the dream prophetic? Is Alejandro still alive? Or is being in La Perlita messing with my overactive mind?

Alejandro's house—the house where he had lived with his mother, stepfather, and brother—is only a block away. His girlfriend, Maria, and son, Nando, had also lived in that small brick house until four months before Alejandro went missing.

I climb the stairs and cross the dining room to the kitchen to make coffee.

Fifteen minutes later, the comforting aroma wafts across my senses as I clutch the hot, red mug. My heart is still hurting from the dream. I sit on my balcony and watch the sunrise. After two strong cups of coffee laden with sweetener and creamer, my head is clearer and my resolve is fortified. I'm ready to find out what happened that fateful day, June 12, 2017. But I need some backup. It's time to contact my "margarita gals."

Before sunset, I head into town to meet my girlfriends. It's a fifteen-minute walk that takes me down the dirt street in front of my house to the main cobblestone road of the neighborhood where I live. The houses and small storefronts in this rural area of La Perlita are mostly modest and poorly constructed. Pickup trucks pass me by, as do bicycles, motorcycles, and horses. I receive waves, smiles, and greetings which I return with, *"Buenas tardes."*

I leave the neighborhood, known as the *barrio,* minutes later and stroll through a subdivision of four hundred upscale dwellings painted in various shades of yellows, oranges, and browns. These places have newer cars behind locked gates and wrought-iron fences. Entertainment areas atop second floors give many of them ocean views. I know most of these folks from Canada and the United States. Like me, they escape cold winters up north and are as friendly as can be.

When I bought my land back in the mid-eighties for a few thousand dollars, this subdivision was sparsely populated and the price of a lot was, and continues to be, ten times more than what I paid.

Leaving the subdivision, I move along a paved road that takes me into the center of town. Two blocks further, the road breaks into three streets running north and south—the beach street on my right, the lagoon street on the left and the main road I'm currently on, which eventually segues into the lagoon street. Turning right at the church, I'm soon at the Oasis Bar on the beach.

There are four of us women who have been enjoying margaritas and sunsets on the beach at this open-air bar for over five years. Joanne, Patty, Estela, and I first met at a Santana tribute band concert in La Perlita's town square. We hooted, hollered, danced, and sang the lyrics until the music stopped at midnight. We agreed to meet the next evening at sunset and sealed the pledge of a new friendship with a big group hug.

Every Wednesday, six months a year since then, we have met to share our joys and sorrows—and to figure out solutions to each other's and the world's problems.

I arrive early to see Joanne already at our table on the beach. She is laughing with the handsome, young waiter, Luis, who has a friendly smile, even white teeth, and an earring in his right ear.

Joanne is a retired dentist from Texas. She looks alluring in a turquoise sundress that accents her blue-green eyes, hugs her voluptuous body, and shows off her honey-brown tan and thick silver-blonde hair. I've always admired how classy she looks at almost sixty-five. She sees me and waves. Her dozen or so silver bracelets clink together like a wind chime.

Before I can approach, I feel a hand on my shoulder and turn to see Patty and Estela right behind me. The long hug feels good and is just what I need. I have missed these women.

"The usual, ladies?" the bar owner asks with a grin that shows a dimple in his left cheek.

"That's a yes for me," I say, embracing Rafael. I've known Rafael since we were teenagers, so many years ago. Back when his father, Pedro, owned this beach bar and my own father, Ernie, shared tequila shots with him. May they both rest in peace.

"But go easy on the tequila, Rafa. It's early in the season. I need to work my way up to a full-dose margarita."

Estela and Patty signal that they will have their usual as well.

Joanne rises from her plastic chair, and we cross over the tiled dance floor and descend two wooden steps to the beach level. There are more embraces and cheek kisses all around, peppered with exclamations of how much we have missed each other. We have six months of catching up ahead of us. We settle in, take off our shoes, and burrow our feet into the warm white sand.

"Thank God!" Patty sighs heavily.

We all laugh, knowing exactly how she feels. It is nice to be together again.

"*Gracias*," we say, as Luis delivers our drinks with a broad smile. He places napkins and a plate of salted peanuts on the table.

I raise my glass. "*Salud.* Here's to another season of fun in the sun and friendship."

"*Salud*," my friends say.

Joanne lives here year-round now, which explains her beautiful tan. Estela, tall and slender, has straight ebony hair that reaches her waist. She was born and raised in this village, although she attended high school and college in Los Angeles. I have been back in town two days and Patty, whom I affectionately think of as "Patita" because of her short stature, arrived yesterday from Canada.

"I thought November would never arrive," I say. "I packed my suitcases back in September and then counted the days to my flight."

"Me, too!" Patty says. Her big smile shows the gap between her front teeth, reminding me of Madonna.

We spend nearly an hour getting caught up on our off-season lives. We share how our children are progressing in their adult lives and lament that we are old enough to be grandmothers.

Joanne touches up her lipstick. "I used to think sixty-five was so old. Now I'm sure it's the new forty."

If only that were true, I think. I join my friends in a toast to the fantasy.

The Oasis Bar fills with locals and tourists as the sun begins to set. As a foursome, we take off our sunglasses and squint, waiting for the green flash that is supposed to appear when the sun dips behind the horizon.

"I missed it again!" I say, dismayed. "Why can't I ever see it?"

Patty straightens in her chair and stomps her feet. "I think it's a hoax. I've never seen it, either. Maybe we have to be really drunk to see the flash."

Estela signals for Luis. "Another round, please."

I laugh. "Mineral water for me, unless you three want to carry me home."

"Such a lightweight," Patty teases.

Joanne and Estela assure us that the green sunset phenomenon exists, but I'm not buying it. What follows the non-green flash are breathtaking hues of color—orange, yellow, and red—now painted across the sky, intermingling with streaks of cumulus, cotton-candy cloud formations that create a spectacular panorama of shifting beauty.

"So, I have something to tell you gals," I say, still a bit tipsy from my one margarita.

Three sets of eyes stare in my direction. "I'm on a mission to find out what happened to Alejandro Garcia."

Estela looks at me and then up and down the beach. "Salvador told me he was warned to back off looking into Alejandro's disappearance," she whispers.

Patty's eyes widen. "Really?"

I check to make sure the nearby tables are empty. "Yes; he told me, too, but that will not stop me," I say, feeling empowered by alcohol. "Somebody has to figure this out."

"I searched for him, you know," Estela says. "Joanne did, too. We walked together up and down the coast where Salvador thought he may have washed ashore."

I smile at Estela, loving her kind heart. "I know you did. And, I thank the three of you for your donations. I wish I could have been here, on the ground, for the search."

Patty slumps in her chair and crosses her arms. "I can't believe he was never found."

I let out a big breath, exhaling weeks and months of stress into the cool breeze, praying that the ocean will return the breath with serenity. "I had a dream about Alejandro last night," I say. "It was awful. I felt so hopeless."

"What happened?" they ask in unison.

My friends lean closer, and I fill them in on the dream.

Obviously as touched as I had been, Estela wipes tears from her face. "Wow. So, how do you plan to find out what happened? How can we help?"

I look into the caring faces of trusted friends. "I need a posse—to be like a confidential sounding board. Are you in?"

"You bet," they say.

"Okay then. Let me start by telling you what I know so far."

⤳ FIVE ⤶

Before I can begin, Luis approaches, wipes the table and refills the peanuts. "Anything else, *chicas*?"

"Another mineral water for me," I say.

"One more round for us," Joanne says after checking with Patty and Estela. She watches Luis walk away, clucks her tongue, and says, "He's delectable!"

I laugh and shake my head. "Calm down, cougar. He can't be more than thirty!"

Joanne gives me a sly grin and winks.

Giving up on trying to tame Joanne, I take out the notebook that now lives in my La Perlita beach bag. "I have a list of people I want to talk to," I say. "I've already spoken with the port captain and his assistant. There are nine more names on the list."

After I read off the names, Estela asks, "So, what have you learned so far?"

"The port captain has more boats under his authority than he can handle," I respond. "Not all captains are licensed, and safety isn't a high priority for some owners. I didn't get the chance to ask him what he personally thinks happened to Alejandro...but I will on Friday."

Estela wrinkles her brow. "I've heard negative things about that guy. My Uncle Gilberto owns several *pangas* and leases them. He says Captain Ricardo hardly ever goes down to the docks. He just stays at his office in town and collects money from boat owners coming into port. And when he does call a meeting of the local owners, few show up."

"The port captain isn't at the docks?" Patty asks. "That sounds strange."

"I was surprised, too," I say. "Luckily Salvador told me where to find the office, which is in the subdivision and not far from my house."

After thanking Luis, I take a sip of my water. "I want to like the man. I want to believe he's not corrupt, and that he did his job."

"Why? Because he's tall and looks good in his dress uniform?" Joanne asks, with a big smile.

I sit back in my chair and laugh. "How did you know that?"

"I've seen him at official events like the yearly Blessing of the Fleet in July. And I know you, girlfriend. I figured you'd like that tall, muscled physique...and the absence of a wedding ring."

"Well, I must admit I was a bit impressed. His deep voice *is* kinda sexy, but first things first. If I find out he purposely delayed looking for Alejandro because somebody paid him not to, or if he didn't fulfill his obligations and that caused Alejandro to be lost at sea, I'd rather prosecute than pursue him."

We take a moment to stare out into the ocean. I breathe in the fresh sea breeze and watch the waves lap onto shore. Seagulls swoop, dip and dive. I wish the waves could tell me what they know about Alejandro.

"There's hope of finding Alejandro alive, you know," Estela says. "Fishermen have gone missing from this coast and were found disoriented, malnourished, but alive months later."

"That's right," Patty says, with hope in her voice. "I remember you posting something about that, Rebecca. Is it true or folklore?"

"No, it's true," I say smiling at Estela. "It was Estela who wrote to tell me about it, and I did some research. Three fishermen aboard a 32-foot-long boat, with the engine broken, without sails or rudder, were discovered and rescued between the Tinall and some other islands. They'd been adrift for over nine months. There had initially been five of them out shark hunting. Two, the captain and his assistant, died of starvation, not willing to eat raw food."

"That's horrific," Joanne says. "I also would be hard pressed to eat raw fish. But it's encouraging that three survived. What's the difference between their boat and the *panga* Alejandro was in?"

"Eight feet. Alejandro was in a 24-footer, and according to Francisco, the assistant port captain, *pangas* are designed to stay afloat."

Patty settles back into her chair. "So, three were rescued. That's comforting,"

"The surviving fishermen had traveled five thousand miles," I inform them. "They had crossed the International Date Line before a passing ship rescued them."

Patty looks at the three of us with a hopeful expression. "I pray Alejandro will be found, then."

Estela drums her fingers on the table and purses her lips. "This never should have happened. It's criminal that Captain Martin left him in that *panga* alone. An experienced fisherman would have known how to stay safe until rescued."

I nod. "We should all pray for Alejandro to be found." Lowering my voice, I add, "I don't know how Captain Martin lives with himself making that decision to leave Alejandro alone on the *panga*. And I bet most everybody in towns agrees it was wrong."

I think back to Salvador's anonymous phone call telling him to stop any further search. Now I can't help but wonder if Captain Martin never intended to return for Alejandro. Or, had he returned to find the boat, but Alejandro dead in the water? Was he paid to leave him out there for some reason? The morbid thoughts tie my stomach into knots.

Estela touches my arm. "Rebecca? Are you all right?"

"Yes, I'm sorry. I got caught up in a flurry of thoughts."

"I was asking," she whispers, "if you knew that Captain Martin has relatives who are part of the Jalisco drug cartel?"

The knots in my stomach clench, making it hard to breathe. "No, I had no idea."

"Me either, but it's the newest rumor around town," Estela says.

Dang! This disappearance has become hard enough to unravel without a cartel connection.

ཨ SIX ᚼ

On Thursday at six, I open the door to *"Bici's y Mas."* Salvador greets me with a smile that lights up his eyes.

"Nice place, *Amigo.*"

"*Gracias.*" His bear hug is comforting.

Salvador Montoya is a tall, thirty-five-year-old college graduate, fitness freak, entrepreneur, and my good friend. He's been a restaurant owner, baker, caterer, wildlife expert and now bike rental shop owner.

"How's business?" I ask, checking out the dozen parked bikes, stacks of kayaks, and a sundry of accessories.

We talk about the slow summer business and his hopes for a busy winter.

I browse through marketing brochures. "You're expanding into zip-lining and rock rappelling?"

"*Sí*, and nature hikes."

"Nina obviously created these brochures. They're beautiful. I love the logo with the bikes by the beach at sunset."

Salvador and his girlfriend, Nina, a graphic artist, came to La Perlita five years ago on vacation and, as so many people do, fell in love with the village. They went back to Guadalajara, quit their jobs, packed their belongings, and returned.

Salvador puts the *"Cerrado"* closed sign on the glass front door and turns the lock. Moments later, he returns from the small kitchen, offers me a glass of mango juice over ice, and sits across from me at his desk. "I'm glad you've returned, Rebecca. I've missed you. La Perlita missed you."

"*Gracias.* It's good to be back. I'm refreshed and ready for the new season. And, as you know, I want to find out what happened to Alejandro."

Silence stuffs its way in between us.

Salvador looks into his glass, twirling ice cubes.

I flip through the brochure in my hand, biding my time. "I know, I know, I know," I finally say. "You don't want me looking into his disappearance. I get that. But Salvador, how can I not?"

"It's easy, Rebecca. Just don't."

"That's easier said than done...for me at least. I had drinks with Estela and two other friends last night. She mentioned you told her about the anonymous phone call."

"Yes. I've known her and her family for years. She was here when I got the call."

"Well, Estela told me that Captain Martin has some family member in the Jalisco Cartel. Is that true?"

Salvador looks out the security-barred store window and back at me. "That's what people say. I haven't verified it. I wouldn't know how to verify it, but I expect it's true. The fact that Martin wasn't jailed for criminal negligence is a telling sign he has somebody on his side. I wanted Lalo, that third fishermen, jailed until he told the police what he saw. But that didn't happen, either."

"The port captain says he filed a complaint against Martin."

"Apparently. And Rosy wrote up one as well—although she hasn't filed it yet."

"So, what happened with the port captain's filing?"

"Nothing."

I shake my head in frustration. "Why?"

"I don't know. I'm hoping Rosy will file hers."

Salvador explains how he helped Rosy write her grievance with all the details of when her son went missing—when she was informed, and how the family tried to get assistance from the authorities, but help was delayed. "She named the port captain, Martin, and Nicolas Vargas in the complaint."

"Who's Nicolas Vargas?"

"The head of a big fishing co-op in La Perlita and the owner of the boat Captain Martin was using."

"Oh, geez. I know that guy...but by his nickname, *Botas*. He's got money." I say. "He owns the big empty lot in the barrio and let me use it one year for a cultural festival. Is he corrupt? Could he have slowed the investigation or covered something up?"

"Possibly. *Pangas* are expensive. A used one can cost three thousand dollars. And the motor is about that same price. That's a lot of pesos invested. You would think he and his buddies would have been all over the ocean to get his *panga* back, with or without Alejandro."

My heart sinks in despair, and I brush a tear off my cheek. "What happened to Alejandro, Salvador? None of this makes sense."

We sit in silence for a few moments, lost in our own thoughts.

After staring out the window again, Salvador looks back at me with concern. "I did hear something of concern," he says in a quiet voice. "Some six years ago, when Alejandro was sixteen and lived in Guadalajara, he was mixed up with drug dealers up there. Something happened, and a cartel member died. I don't know the details. Alejandro left there in a hurry and came here to live with his mother. He changed his life and had nothing to do with gangs, or drugs, or anything. But apparently the cartel doesn't forget, and some say they ordered his death that day out in the *panga.*"

I shake my head in disbelief. "No way. Six years later? Six years later someone orders Alejandro killed? Sweet, caring Alejandro?"

"Rebecca, do you remember when Cesar jumped on a bus to Guadalajara during the first days of the search?"

"*Sí.* He sent me a text from the bus. He needed to follow up on a lead he received from his uncle about Alejandro. He didn't say what."

"Well, what I have just told you in confidence is the 'what.'"

ᵔ SEVEN ᵔ

Friday morning at eleven, I walk into the Port Captaincy building. Francisco greets me and I take a seat. *"Buenos días, Señorita* Rebecca. *Capitán* Ricardo is running late. He'll be with you shortly."

This does not surprise me. Taking out the small mirror from my bag, I check my face, use fingers to fluff up my curls, refresh my lipstick, and settle in to review my notes. I live on "gringo time," a bit ahead of "Mexican time." My friends say they will arrive at eleven and waltz in at noon as if they're being punctual. Living in Mexico as a North American demands a few adjustments. People and relations are more important than activity. Time does not equate to money. Family comes first. I've made plenty of adjustments over the years, but still don't like to be late for any appointment.

Captain Ricardo comes through the front doors at eleven thirty. "Rebecca. *Me alegro verte. Adelante.*"

"Gracias. It's nice to see you, too," I say, somewhat surprised by his friendly tone.

We give each other a quick hug. He's not in uniform and I secretly admire his tight Levi's and white, tailored short-sleeved shirt. He gestures for me to walk ahead of him to his office.

Inviting me to sit, the captain gets comfortable in his chair and begins to straighten the piles of documents on his desk. "Sorry I'm a bit late. Abby and Annie didn't want me to leave the house this morning. They are such babies. I spent some extra moments cuddling them before coming into the office." His proud parental smile overtakes his face and brings a sparkle to his brown eyes.

"How old are your children?" I ask, mentally scratching his name off my list of possible eligible bachelors.

"*Niños*? My children are grown and on their own, living near my ex-wife in Mexico City. Abby and Annie are my twin poodles."

Alarms go off in my body. I like dogs, but am distrustful of men who are overly attached to theirs. Oh, please don't be one of *those* men, I pray. I keep a smile on my face and suspend judgment for now.

"I made some phone calls since our last meeting," the port captain says.

I redirect my wandering mind. "Phone calls about what?"

"To find out what happened with the complaint I filed against Captain Martin."

"And?"

"He was never arrested or charged with a crime."

I'm only three minutes into our meeting and my stomach is churning. "*¿Por qué no?*"

"I don't know why."

He explains how he writes up infractions, the police department decides to charge or not, and the investigative unit then looks into the complaint, submitting their recommendation. They will indict if warranted.

"What were your charges?" I ask.

"Unsafe working conditions. Criminal negligence."

My mind swirls. "Is it unusual for Captain Martin to have gotten off without any consequences?"

"*Sí*. I expected he would at least be arrested. Maybe the matter is still being investigated."

"After five months?"

"It could be."

I sit back in my chair. "Hmmm. Is it possible that somebody was paid off to not arrest Captain Martin and not look into what happened to Alejandro?"

"Anything is possible. I would hope not, but corruption is everywhere. It's out of my hands now."

"What happened when you levied the fine against Nicolas Vargas?"

"Botas? He paid up. *No problema*. He took responsibility for that *panga* leaving port with no safety equipment on board, even though the blame should have been on Captain Martin."

I want to scream, but steady my voice. "Why is Captain Martin getting away with possible murder?"

"There are rumors, but I'm not at liberty to discuss them."

"Do you mean the rumors about one of his relatives being a member of the cartel?"

Captain Ricardo's eyes show his shock at my question. He pauses. "As I said, I'm not at liberty to discuss rumors."

I pause and look at the notes I've collected so far. "Okay, so your complaint against Martin hasn't gone anywhere. What if the family files charges? Would that hurry along the investigation?"

"It might. They haven't, so far that I know. But they have three years to do so." The captain leans towards me and chuckles. "You're relentless in your questions, *Señorita* Rebecca. What else do you have in that notebook of yours?"

I give him a slight smile and ready my next question. "So, what do you think happened to Alejandro?"

Captain Ricardo shakes his head, settles into his leather chair and absently touches the side of his close-cropped mustache with his index finger. "Francisco and I have discussed this over and over. We believe he was blown off course that night in the storm and drifted west, which is the direction the wind pattern and current would have taken him."

"West, toward where?"

He pulls out a nautical chart and pushes it across the desk so we can both see it. "This is where Martin says he left him," showing me a spot off the coast of Jalisco, near the state line of Nayarit. "The GPS coordinates placed him north, by a massive rock formation known as 'White Rock,' which is near Nuevo Vallarta beach, right here."

I gaze up and down the Mexican shoreline and notice the miles and miles of ocean to the west. "Here's the beach, but I don't see any white rock."

"It's not on the chart. It's a landmark the fishermen know. It's located a half mile off the beach," he says, moving his finger from right to left. "The current, along with the strong easterly winds that night, would have sent him out into the middle of the ocean, heading west."

"Let me see if I understand. The coast of Mexico is here," I say, pointing on the map to the North American land mass. "And if the wind and current take him due west, he would end up...way over here in the Philippines, or near the Marshall Islands?"

"Theoretically. But that's very far away."

I check the chart closely. "It's almost twice as far as Hawaii."

"Yes, it is. There are a few scattered islands here and there, but not a lot of land between Mexico and the Philippines."

Taking a tissue out of my bag, I dab a perspiration spot on my temple, trying not to remove my foundation, and hope the captain doesn't notice. I then ask him about fishermen known to have survived months adrift in the Pacific.

"*Sí*. Three men were rescued by a Marshall Islands fishing vessel in Kiribati waters, in 2006. They had been drifting for nearly ten months. More recently, in 2014, a man from El Salvador, living in Mexico, went shark fishing with a friend. The motor failed. He drifted for 438 days before floating into a small island of the Ebon Atoll. There had originally been two on the small boat, but one died."

We spend a few minutes talking about these tragic incidences and looking at the chart. He shows me Ebon Atoll and nearby Kiribati, neither of which I've ever heard of.

"Ebon Atoll is a coral atoll of twenty-two islands in the Pacific Ocean, forming part of the Marshall Islands. See how it's located northeast of Australia, between Australia and Hawaii?" He marks the area with his forefinger.

I nod.

"Its land area is only 2.2 square miles," he explains.

"That's all? 2.2 square miles? Are the islands inhabited?"

"Four of the islets have people on them. The larger, Ebon Island, has a medical center, I believe."

I dab another drop of perspiration, this time from my neck, and Captain Ricardo picks up his desk phone. "Francisco, turn on the air conditioner, and bring Rebecca a glass of cold water, *por favor.*"

I reward Ricardo with a big smile. "So there's hope for Alejandro, *sí*?" I feel optimistic about Alejandro's chance of survival and pleased by the captain's attention.

"Unfortunately, no. At least I don't think so. Alejandro had no experience at sea. From what I've been told there was nothing on board the *panga* except a large piece of material used as a blanket on chilly mornings and a paddle."

His words break my heart and I feel pressure behind my eyes. I don't want to cry in front of this man, even though I'm starting to trust him—somewhat.

"Could it have been a cover-up?" I ask. "Is it possible that Captain Martin returned to find him dead and concealed the death?"

"That's pretty far-fetched, Rebecca. Alejandro was young and healthy. You don't die after a few hours of sun exposure."

"You're right." Bracing myself, I ask a question that has been nagging at me for months. "Is it possible his death was ordered, and his body hidden or pushed overboard, tied to an anchor?"

Captain Ricardo leans forward in his chair, rests clasped hands on the desk, and stares at me. "Who would want him dead? Do you know something I don't?"

Francisco enters the office with my glass of water—pausing our conversation. *"Gracias,"* I say, grateful for the few moments of respite.

"Not for certain," I finally respond. "But people are talking. We can't figure out why a body never washed to shore. Obviously, there's speculation."

"And what about the boat?" he asks. "*Pangas* with motors are too expensive for a captain to just sink it to the ocean floor."

I stare at my notebook and then look at him. "Well, one thought is the boat was brought back into port under the cover of darkness. It was sanded down, repainted, and given a new name."

"Rebecca. Who is filling your head with such rumors? If a new boat is placed in service in La Perlita it must be registered with this office and no new *panga* has been registered, nor seen."

I feel the captain's frustration, but I don't want to reveal that friends and acquaintances have been sending me messages with possible theories for months, so I ask another question. "Could it have been carted off and resold at another port?"

Captain Ricardo sits back and crosses his arms. He doesn't answer right away, so we sit in silence for a few moments. I feel my heart racing and can hear Francisco talking to somebody down the hall.

"I can't help you on that subject. I'm not connected to that world. And if there was a hit ordered, I'd suggest you stop playing detective."

His words surprise me. Is he warning me because he cares?—that's flattering—or is he threatening me to stay away?—that's scary. Is he really not connected to that world? I want to trust him. Can I? Should I?

❧ EIGHT ❧

Last night, hours after my meeting with Captain Ricardo, I lay awake watching the clock tick tock closer to sunrise. I used the time to review what I know so far, which is essentially nothing. My head and notebook hold a lot of theories, possibilities, fears, and rumors, but few facts—except that Alejandro went out fishing and didn't return.

I had stopped by Alejandro's house after my meeting with the port captain and left a message for Rosy that I'd like to see her. Her husband promised to give her my message. Thinking about her pain makes my mother's heart want to cry.

I must have fallen asleep just before dawn because I had another Alejandro dream.

This time I was in the *panga*, but he couldn't see me. I watched him look at the dark clouds directly overhead and shudder. He didn't seem prepared for the surge that pushed ahead of the storm. The waves took on new force, slamming against the *panga's* side like angry surf on a beach. They washed repeatedly over the boat. It was all he could do to stay onboard.

I could tell the motion made him dizzy. I wanted to hug him and say, "Hang on."

His face brightened. We felt the cooling drops of rain. *Rain!*

Alejandro grabbed the bench for support and held up an empty water bottle. At the same time, he opened his mouth to catch whatever drops would fall inside.

I watched him untie the back two sides of the shade fabric and wring it dry, ridding it of saltwater. He then elevated it above his head so rain would soak in.

A wave approached and I screamed at him to watch out.

He did, keeping hold of both the material and the bench.

Every few minutes he squeezed the material to capture dribbles of water into the plastic bottle. He managed to fill it once, gulped it down immediately, and then repeated the process.

When the storm finally passed, it was dark. No stars. No moon. Just the endless pitching and rocking of the boat. The blanket stayed damp. I watched as Alejandro shivered and prayed in the cold. He did not sleep.

I awake with "rain" running down my cheeks.

Last night's dream stays with me all morning, and I wonder if I'm getting too close to this investigation. Maybe I should take Salvador's and the port captain's advice and stop peering into handfuls of sand, hoping to find nuggets of gold.

I decide to stay home today, to putter in the garden and relax in the cool water of my swimming pool. To enjoy anything right now, however, is difficult. How can I be joyful when a young man is either dead or maybe floating, alone, somewhere in the open ocean?

I take a deep yoga cleansing breath and pray for God to provide Alejandro's family, friends, and me a peace that is beyond understanding. And I pray that Rosy will stop by to see me.

My doorbell rings around ten o'clock. I look down from my balcony to see Rosy, standing outside the privacy wall. She holds a young boy by the hand. Alejandro's son, Nando?

"*Buenos días.* I'll be right there."

I hurry down the outside staircase and rush to the front courtyard door. "Come in. *Adelante.* It's so good to see you."

"I heard you were back, Rebecca, and got the message you stopped by."

"*Sí,* I arrived on Monday. *Siéntese, por favor.*" I lead her and the young boy to the love seat and chairs placed under the awning by the pool. "Is this Nando?"

"*Sí.* Nando, say hello to *Señora* Rebecca."

Nando looks at me and I see a faint smile. He looks like Alejandro with those big brown eyes. He was just learning to walk when I last saw him. I remember Alejandro's proud-daddy smile as he held out his arms, encouraging Nando to toddle to him. He then lifted him up high and held him close to his chest. The memory brings tears to my eyes.

Nando turns to glance at the swimming pool as Rosy combs her fingers through his hair, moving errant strands into place.

"How old is he now?" I ask.

"*Tiene dos años.*"

"He's small for two," I say. "*Hola, Nando. ¿Como estás?*"

He gives me another faint smile, crawls into his grandmother's lap, and lays his head against her chest.

"He's pretty shy...and it's his nap time," she explains.

Rosy is in her mid-forties but looks ten years older. Grief and years of her struggles with drugs have etched marks on her face. She is dressed in a dark-blue sleeveless blouse and blue jeans ripped at the knees. Her curly black hair, streaked with gray, spirals in every direction.

I ask if she has custody of Nando now and she shares that Maria, Nando's mother, lets her have him several days a week.

"She wanted to take Nando and move out of town with her new boyfriend. I begged her not to. I've lost my son. I can't lose my grandson, too."

My heart hurts for her. It's such a sad situation. "How are you doing, Rosy?"

"I'm dying inside," she says. "People don't understand the pain of losing a child. Not knowing where he is. I can't sleep or eat. I feel so lost. When I do sleep for a few minutes, I see him. I want to save him and can't. It crushes me..."

I move my chair closer and caress her arm. "I'm so sorry."

"I've become paralyzed by my anger against Martin. I hate him. He didn't even tell me my son was missing. I found out at the corner grocery store."

"I remember you telling me that when we spoke on the phone during the search. That's just cruel."

Rosy looks toward the palm trees in the courtyard, lost in thought. "My phone rang when I was at the store. It was Alejandro's friend, Javier. He asked me about Ale, I guess to see what I knew, and I told him he was still out fishing. But after a moment, Javi tells me Alejandro is lost at sea. I slammed shut the phone. I couldn't talk. I couldn't move. I'm his mother and I didn't know."

Tears roll down her cheeks and drop onto Nando's loose brown curls.

"I'm so sorry," is all I can think to say.

"I grabbed my bicycle and rode to Martin's mother's house. I asked her where her son lived so I could confront him. She told me Martin was out looking for Alejandro. When I asked her why he hadn't come to tell me the news, she said he didn't know where I lived. *Mentira!* That's a lie. He had been to my house at least twice to pick Ale up for work...." Her voice trails off and I fight back my tears.

Rosy, her husband, and sons live one street west. I'm closer to her sons, Cesar and Alejandro, than to her. Her daughter, Perla, lives in a nearby city. They're a good, kind, sometimes-financially struggling family. Rosy stops by on occasion to ask for money for a variety of reasons, from buying medicine to paying an overdue light bill.

"What did Martin tell you when you finally talked to him?"

"He said he left Alejandro alone for a couple of hours while he went to pull in the long-line and when he returned, Ale and the *panga* were gone."

"That's what he told the port captain, too," I say.

She hugs Nando, who has fallen asleep. "That damn port captain. It's his fault my son is missing."

Her statement shocks me. "The port captain's fault? Why?"

"Because he let Martin leave port without any safety equipment onboard the *panga*. That's his responsibility. He is corrupt and didn't act quickly enough to find Alejandro."

I remain silent. I understand how Captain Ricardo's hands had been tied during those first hours. He wasn't present at 3:30 in the morning when Martin and his crew left the dock. When notified of the disappearance later that evening, it was too late to do anything. He filed a report Tuesday morning, but then protocol set in to determine jurisdiction. I couldn't speak to corruption. But, as a friend to this family and as a mother myself, I don't think "protocol" should come before immediate life-saving action.

"I prayed over him late that night...hours before he left to go fishing. I prayed that they would catch lots of fish and that God and the *Santísima Virgen María* would protect him." Rosy begins to sob and I embrace her, wanting to shelter her and Nando from this tragedy.

I wait for the sobs to subside. "Are you going to be all right? Is there anything I can do?"

She takes a deep breath and wipes her tears. "Thank you, but no. You've done so much. Thank you for telling the public about Alejandro's disappearance and pushing for the search-and-rescue effort. I will always be grateful to you, and Salvador, and others in town who helped us search."

I take Rosy's hand and give it a squeeze. "I'm so sorry we didn't find him."

She nods and her eyes drop before rising to meet mine again. "I think Alejandro is still alive." She pauses and then says, "I haven't told anybody."

Surprised by her words, I sit back in my chair. "What do you mean?"

Rosy gently rocks Nando. "I went to the village of Sebastian to see a psychic. He told me."

"What did he say?"

"He said Alejandro is warm and cared for. That he's not hungry."

My heart pounds as my mind swirls with concern. I'm personally skeptical of psychics, but people do claim to have that ability. Psychic-based crime solvers are not a new phenomenon, but I hope for Rosy's sake this is real and not a scam to take money from a grieving mother. "Did he give you his location?"

Rosy hesitates. "I took him one of Ale's shirts. He held onto it and we waited. He seemed to struggle at first to get through to him. Then he saw Alejandro—safe—but couldn't tell me where. He told me to come back."

"Are you going to see him again?"

"Probably. I have to save some money. It's a long way away...up in the Sierra Madre Mountains."

"Do you believe what he told you?"

"A mother knows when her child is dead. I can't bury the memory of my son because I think he's alive somewhere. I can feel it, Rebecca. I have faith. I don't tell people this because they'll think I'm crazy or back on drugs. But I'm not."

I'm speechless. My heart reaches out to this distraught mother. I refuse to do or say anything to dissuade her from believing she'll see her son again.

We sit in silence and watch Nando begin to stir.

"I pray you and the psychic are right. I really do."

⇜ NINE ⇝

On Monday, a week after my arrival, my niece Lisa and I enter the *Paraiso* for a late lunch. It's one of three open-air restaurants on a short street that runs parallel to the La Perlita lagoon. Fishermen pull up daily to the restaurant dock, tie off, and unload fresh catch.

"I haven't been here yet this season. Have you?" I ask.

"No. It seemed weird. Alejandro was always a welcoming face and now he's gone."

I nod. "Perhaps we need to get used to that."

Carmen, Paraiso's owner, greets us. "Rebecca and Lisa, you're back. Welcome,"

I stoop to give Carmen a hug and kiss on her cheek. Lisa follows suit. In her late forties, Carmen looks and dresses like a twenty-something. Today she has on cropped Levi's, ruby-red canvas wedge sandals showing off her scarlet-painted toenails, and an embroidered red-and-white peasant blouse. Her long, dark hair is braided and hangs over her right shoulder.

"It's so good to see you. Can we have a table under a fan?" I ask.

Carmen laughs and gives me one of her delightful smiles showing perfect white teeth. She leads us to a table on the lagoon side, under a large, swirling fan.

"You've replaced the roof," I say. "It looks great."

"*Gracias*," she says, before leaving us to attend to another customer.

A dozen Mexican flags hang from the new *palapa* thatched roof made of tight-fitting dried palm leaves. Decorative piñatas and light fixtures made from woven reed provide a cultural festive ambience. Mariachi music plays softly in the background and the smells of onions, garlic, and chili dance from the kitchen through the restaurant on the slightest of a breeze.

Settling in, we scan the menu. Carmen's son José comes over. He sets a portable fan on a nearby chair and turns it to high.

"Thank you, José." I rise to greet him with an embrace, grateful he always remembers my need for an extra fan during these sweltering months.

José is the type of young man a mother would want her daughter to marry—handsome, educated, and hardworking, with impeccable manners.

"How's university?" I ask. "Have you finish your degree?"

"Almost. One more semester and I'll have my bachelor's in business with a minor in tourism."

"That's wonderful. Congratulations," I say.

Lisa orders white wine and I ask for mineral water on ice with a slice of lemon.

I look around and take a deep breath. "It's good to be back."

"I agree," Lisa says.

Moments later, José returns, carrying a platter with our drinks, chips and salsa, and an appetizer. "Marlin in mango sauce. Compliments of the house."

"*Gracias,*" we say in unison.

Lisa orders a chicken and beef *molcajete,* a signature dish at the *Paraiso*—tender meat and vegetables baked in a lava bowl with a seasoned-to-order red sauce. I ask for a shrimp salad and tortilla soup, delicious even in hot weather.

Savoring the surroundings for a moment, I gaze out the back of the restaurant to the immense fresh-water lagoon and take a deep calming breath. This spacious water mass separates La Perlita, which is in the state of Jalisco, from Las Brisas, a small town on the state of Nayarit side.

A white egret with a four-foot wingspan swoops down and lands on a *panga* beached on the sand next to the restaurant. I watch passengers load into a boat taxi at the nearby dock—most likely on their way to work or to eat at one the restaurants in Las Brisas, just a ten-minute ride away. Being so close, the two beach towns routinely share workers and patrons.

"A toast to my mom and how blessed we are to call this village home."

"Amen to that."

Lisa takes a sip of wine and adjusts her dark rimmed glasses—which always seem to fall forward, making her look like a stern librarian.

After placing our orders with the chef, José returns along with Carmen to sit at our table. We exchange small talk about our lives off-season and then I bring up the subject I really want to discuss. "Has anything new surfaced about Alejandro?"

José speaks first. "Not that I know of. At least, I haven't heard anything. What a tragedy."

"Do you have a theory?" I ask.

"I think the *panga* drifted away from where they left him, and waves from the big storm overturned the boat."

I tilt my head and look at José. "And the *panga*? Why didn't it wash up on shore?"

"It might have, and somebody stole it," he says.

"Hmmm...possible, I guess. What do you think happened?" I ask Carmen.

Carmen looks at her son and then at me. She seems hesitant to give an opinion, so I try the appetizer, compliment her on the dish, and wait.

"I think he's still alive somewhere," Carmen finally says.

"Alive? Why do you think that?" Lisa asks, shock in her voice.

I haven't told Lisa about Rosy and the psychic. I wonder if Carmen went to consult one as well.

Carmen lowers her voice. "A friend in Bucerías told me Alejandro was seen that same evening walking through the town square."

"I've heard a lot of theories, Carmen, but that's a new one," I say.

José looks at me and shakes his head. "I don't believe that, Rebecca, but my mom is convinced." Seeing customers at the front of the restaurant, he excuses himself and leaves.

Lisa and I look at each other and I shrug my shoulders. "Anything is possible. Bucerías is just up the coast and that *is* where his new girlfriend lives."

"Why do you believe that could be true?" Lisa asks Carmen.

Carmen looks around as if to make sure no customers are seated nearby and lowers her voice. "I had to fire Alejandro, right after New Year's. He hadn't been showing up for work, and New Year's Day, which is one of our busiest, he came into work drunk."

I shake my head. "That doesn't sound like the Alejandro I know."

"He was devastated when Maria left him," Carmen continues. "She already had a new boyfriend and took their baby and moved in with the new guy."

"I knew about the breakup. And heard rumors about a new guy," I say. "I didn't know if I should believe it and never asked."

I sit back and cross my legs. "Poor Alejandro. And, I had no idea you fired him, Carmen. The times I came in here to eat and didn't see him, I assumed it was his day off."

"He changed," Carmen says. "He drank. A lot."

I look at Lisa and then Carmen. "His mom and brother told me about his girlfriend, Luisa. Salvador sent me a copy of the last text Alejandro sent her. The port captain or Salvador got it from the girl."

Carmen lowers her voice again and I lean in. "She wasn't his only girlfriend. There were several, and one of the new conquests...he stole from a local cartel member."

"No way!" Lisa almost chokes on her drink and her glasses fall to the tip of her nose. Her disbelief echoes my own sentiment.

"From the time I fired him in January until he disappeared in June, he spent his time collecting girlfriends, drinking, getting people angry at him, and running up debts," Carmen says. "At least those are the rumors. I myself believe them."

I'm not convinced and refuse to see Alejandro through that lens. "Is there any proof?"

Carmen remains adamant. "Some of it. Many in town, including me, saw him drunk and with different women. You know how small La Perlita is. Things don't stay secret for long."

In Alejandro's defense, I can understand why a good-looking twenty-two-year-old, abandoned by the mother of his child, would start playing the field. "That's almost human nature," I say. "Come to think of it, his mom did tell me, back in July, that Alejandro left behind a lot of unpaid bills, which she's paying off."

Lisa dips a chip into the fresh salsa. "I don't know if I believe that theory," she says. "I can't see Alejandro leaving behind his son. Auntie, didn't you tell me he went fishing that day to earn money for Nando's baptism ceremony?"

"Yes. I heard that from both his mom and brother."

Carmen prepares to leave as our lunch arrives. "Thank you, Carmen, for sharing your thoughts," I say. "It may be true; we just don't know. Somebody with a boat would have had to pull the disabled *panga* into a remote area where they wouldn't be seen. Maybe that person gave him money for the boat so he could run away. But to where? The girlfriend is still in Bucerías, so she didn't go with him."

"Not only that," Lisa adds, "he didn't know the motor was going to fail and that Captain Martin was going to leave him alone in the boat. If he did orchestrate an escape from his problems, he would have had to do so on the fly."

✌ TEN ✌

Wednesday evening has arrived and I'm excited to meet up with my margarita gals. Even though I see them around town individually, this is our official girls' night.

We are hardly in our chairs when Estela places her elbows on the table, cradles her face in her hands, and says, "Well...?"

I chuckle at her rapt attention. "I have lots to tell you. But let's get our drinks first."

We repeat our ritual of shoes off, toes in the sand, chitter-chatter, and when Luis approaches we place our orders. "The usual, please."

"I'm dying to hear," Estela says. "I know you've been talking to people because people are saying you're asking around."

"So much for being covert," I say.

"Aren't you afraid?" Patty asks, looking nervous. "I've been thinking you should stop. I'm afraid for you. You don't know what you're going to find or who you might piss off."

"Stop? I just got started. Afraid for asking questions? No. I'm just a *gringa* wondering what happened to my friend Alejandro."

Patty shakes her head. "Be careful, Rebecca. Please."

We glance around to make sure the other tables on the beach are still unoccupied. Our cautious glances make me laugh aloud. "We're acting like we're in the middle of an Agatha Christie murder mystery," I say to lighten the mood.

"It kinda is. Isn't it?" Patty asks.

"It's a mystery for sure. I don't know yet if it was murder—I'm hoping it wasn't."

Luis arrives with our drinks. My margarita tastes sweet, cool and refreshing. Just the way I like it.

"So? What did you find out?" Estela asks.

Out comes my notebook. "In a nutshell, nobody seems to know what happened that day. And if they do, they're not telling me. Alejandro's mom went to a psychic, who told her he's still alive. Carmen, from the *Paraiso* restaurant, says he was seen in Bucerías the evening he went missing. So that's two for believing he's still alive. Carmen's son, José, thinks it was an accident—Alejandro drowned, the boat washed ashore, and somebody stole it."

I take a deep breath, thinking of all the possibilities, and add, "And, if the rumor that he started dating the girlfriend of a drug dealer is true, it's possible he was killed for that."

"Wow. Psychic? Still alive? Those seem far-fetched," Joanne says.

"Murdered? Geez! What about Salvador?" Patti asks. "What does he think?"

"He's not committing to anything but holds onto the possibility Alejandro was killed—that the cartel ordered his death. Which is the only plausible reason for the anonymous phone call he received."

Joanne takes a sip of her margarita and sets her glass on the table. "This isn't some big city. We live in a small fishing village. Cartel hits aren't supposed to happen here."

Estela lowers her voice to a whisper. "They shouldn't... but they do. Do you remember six years ago, when Toro was murdered by a hitman?"

Estela and Joanne turn toward me. Toro, a high-level drug dealer representing the now nearly defunct *La Familia* cartel, had moved in next door to me, disrupting my paradise. A couple of years later, a new group attempted to take over the drug-selling zones up and down the coast. Hitmen, known as *sicarios*, assassinated Toro in the process. I had come to care about Toro and his young family, and my heart still hurts over his murder and the disappearance of his wife.

"That was back before you started spending your winters here, Patty," I explain, touching her arm. "Drugs are dealt in almost every town in the world. La Perlita is no exception. It's an underground mafia world that drug-free people don't usually see. Although it is possible that a contract was put out on Alejandro for something he did in Guadalajara years ago or for dating the girlfriend of a cartel member...there's no evidence that that's what happened."

"You lived next door to a cartel member and never mentioned it?" Patty asks, concern on her face.

"It's a long story. I don't often talk about it. But what I learned from the experience is that men...or women... in the cartel were first 'people' before becoming 'cartel members.'"

We sit for a moment, each lost in our own thoughts. "How did your meeting with the port captain go?" Joanne finally asks. "Any breakthroughs?"

Wanting to change the conversation to something a bit more light-hearted, I joke, "He's still handsome in a distinguished kind of way. But...he has dogs!"

Suppressing a grin, I take a swig of my drink. The four of us look at each other and begin to chuckle, then laugh, and then belly laugh until blended strawberry margarita threatens to come out my nose.

"Oh, no!" Joanne says, raking manicured nails through her long hair. "That's terrible for you."

Estela's smile lights up her face. "Are you ever going to get over your boyfriend-and-his-dog trauma?"

My ex-partner had caressed and spoken love talk to his dog ad nauseam—with me sitting right in the room, feeling ignored. "I don't think so! I don't intend to be the third wheel again!"

"We know, we know, you poor thing," Estela says.

"But that doesn't mean Captain Ricardo is that way. Maybe he loves his dogs but doesn't use them to fill an emotional void," Patty offers.

"What else did you find out?" Joanne asks. "Does the captain have a girlfriend?"

"I don't know about a girlfriend, but he's divorced, with adult children who live in Mexico City."

Joanne smiles. "That's good...so are you going to hook up with him?"

Joanne's question doesn't surprise me, coming from her. She went through a devastating divorce six years ago, that left her feeling old, unattractive, and unlovable. She recreated herself here in La Perlita as a rich, classy vixen and is now all about living life to the fullest, including falling in and out of love and beds. I don't judge her life choices, but I'm not that free."

"Slow down, girlfriend. It's not an impossibility, but I need to get to know him better," I say. "We'll see. I sense he feels bad about the time it took to start looking for

Alejandro. He doesn't buy into it being a cartel hit, or at least he's not admitting that to me. Unless investigators compel Captain Martin to talk, we may never know."

Estela turns serious. "From talk around the port, the police have spoken to Martin and to Lalo, the other fisherman on board that day. Both of them keep telling the same story. They left Alejandro to tend the boat, they returned, and he was gone."

"So now what?" Patty asks. "What's next on your list of things to do? Do you need my help?"

Patty's offer makes me smile. She's petite, fit, with spiky blonde hair, and looks tough with a tattooed cross on her left upper arm. But she spends most of her time in yoga classes and meditating on the beach. Not exactly the "Rambo" type.

"I have no doubt you'd have my back as I go talk to people, *Patita*, but I'm good. If you spoke Spanish, I'd take you along—just for your moxie factor," I tease and smile.

"I speak Spanish," Estela says.

"You definitely do. More than me, even. But because you're a local, it's best for you to not get too involved. I'll call you if I get into any trouble."

"What about me?" Joanne asks with a sly smile, as if she doesn't want to be left out of volunteering.

"Sure. If I find somebody who I think you can break down with your love and passion, I'll text you!"

Sharing a laugh with my girlfriends takes away my angst for only a moment. "But, right now I have four more people on my list. Sergio, from the sports fishing association, Alejandro's brother, and the two guys from the rescuing boat, Alfonso and Beto. And, I'd really like to talk to Martin."

"I doubt that will happen," Estela says. "He's not talking to anybody."

❧ ELEVEN ❧

It's a relaxing Saturday morning. Latin pop songs filter into the yard from the CD player in my bedroom. Lying on an air mattress in the swimming pool, I sing along with Ricky Martin to his song, *Perdóname*.

A loud knock on the courtyard door, followed by the doorbell, interrupts my performance.

"I'll be right there," I shout, wondering who is so impatient to see me.

Ascending the pool steps, I reach for a towel, head to the door and open it a crack. "Cesar, *hola*. Please come in. *Adelante*."

Cesar, Alejandro's older brother, almost stumbles in mid-step. Morose, bloodshot eyes look at me. His stooped shoulders age him.

"Rebecca." Cesar wraps his arms around me, pulling me close.

His sadness engulfs me. "I'm so sorry, Cesar," I whisper into his ear. I smell sweat on his neck and he reeks of alcohol. His prickly face stubble scratches my cheek, but I don't want to break the embrace.

Cesar was the first person I met from the Garcia family. We bonded over a starving dog I'd found on a street corner near my house. I had asked around the neighborhood for the dog's owner and then followed a store manager's directions to a nearby house. Cesar answered my knock. Frida, the Garcias' purebred red Doberman, had birthed a litter of seven pups. Between not being fed properly, and the pups taking nutrients from her starving body, she looked near death.

Over the next several months, the family welcomed me into their home, where I taught them to make dog food from left-over rice, beans, and tortillas mixed with veggies and broth from beef bones donated by the neighborhood butcher. They allowed me to bring the local vet to their home to treat not only Frida but her pups and two other canines on the property. It took patience, several surgeries, and an agreement between the Garcia family and me, which resulted in a healthy, spayed, happy Doberman. The side benefit was my unlikely friendship with the Garcia family and Cesar in particular.

"I'm glad to see you." I take his hand and lead him to the chairs by the pool. His hand feels clammy. "You look terrible," I say. Tall, lanky Cesar is twenty-five, but he seems to have aged terribly since I saw him seven months ago. He looks disheveled—like he had dressed with his eyes shut—wearing a stained white t-shirt and dirty, crumpled Levi's. Tear-filled eyes are the window dressing to his hurt-filled soul.

"Any word?" I ask a few moments later.

"None, *Chula*," he says, using his nickname for me, which means "good looking." "Five months without a word. Without evidence, without Alejandro."

We both stare as a black raven flutters down from a coconut tree onto the top pool step. I watch the bird fluff his feathers and poke his pale beak into the water.

"Some things don't make sense," I offer. "Some things

don't have answers. Maybe we have to accept that about Alejandro."

"No!" Cesar's outburst startles the raven, which flies up over the privacy wall to land on the roof of the two-story house across the street. Cesar brushes unkempt hair out of his eyes. "I'll never accept it, *Chula*. Never. My little brother didn't deserve whatever happened to him. But I want to know what *did* happen."

I stare at him for a few moments before finally releasing my breath. "What do you think happened? I remember you telling me you were heading to Guadalajara to get answers. Did you find any?"

He shakes his head. "No. My uncle thought maybe a cartel member's death by someone in a gang Alejandro was involved in years ago may have caused some type of payback. But we talked to people up there...and there's no word, rumor, or evidence of retaliation."

"How deeply was he involved in that gang and how sure are you that somebody didn't order retribution?"

"I'm sure, Chula. Alejandro was only sixteen at the time. We asked around and found out that the guy who actually killed the cartel member in self-defense is still alive, so why come after my brother?"

"That makes sense. So...what about here?" I ask. "I heard he may have been involved with some guy's girlfriend. Maybe that was it. Or...was he personally involved in something... illegal?"

"You mean the rumor about the cartel guy's girlfriend? I looked into that, too, talking to some dudes I know. They deny it."

I caress his arm in comfort. I personally wouldn't believe the word of a cartel member, but I'm not going to add to his anguish.

Cesar stoops forward and places both elbows on his knees. "There's no way Ale was involved in something illegal. No way.

"Me? Yes. I've been honest with you over the years about selling drugs and stolen merchandise. That's in my past. But not my brother. He prays over his food, Chula. He's a dad. A great father. He did nothing to cause his disappearance. That's what's so crazy!"

Picking up a napkin from the side table, I wipe the perspiration from my neck—perspiration that seems to defy the cooling fan overhead. I watch the raven return to the pool steps and complete his bath. "What else then, Cesar? I'm trying to look into all possible theories."

"I think there was some accident and he died on the *panga* and Martin covered it up."

"Why do you think that?"

"Do you remember the pictures sent from his cell phone? The one of a shade cover he supposedly set up?"

"*Sí.*"

"I think somebody else sent that picture. I think Alejandro was already dead before that picture was sent to his girlfriend."

"Why?"

"Because Alejandro never, ever took a picture without him being in it! He was the king of selfies. Just look at his Facebook page. It's full of pictures, and he's always in them."

I'm intrigued. "What do you think that means, then?"

"I think Martin and the other fishermen returned and found Alejandro's drowned body floating near the *panga*. Maybe he fell overboard, hit his head, and couldn't get back into the boat. They didn't want to get charged with his death."

"And his body? The boat?" I ask, wanting to understand his logic.

"I think they disposed of his body and late that night pulled the *panga* to shore, probably at Bucerías or Punta Mita, and stashed it away."

"So you don't buy into the theory somebody saw him wandering around, disoriented on the beach near Las Brisas?"

"No. We heard the rumor. Friends went with me. We drove over there and searched for hours. Later, someone found a piece of a shirt and swore it was his. My mom looked at it and it wasn't."

Cesar shakes his head. "Someone else found an old piece of fiberglass and said it was from the *panga*. There was no proof of that, either. People—the port captain, Captain Martin, and others—wanted to wrap this all up neat and tidy. It was all a lie. He never came back to shore, Chula."

My heart breaks for Cesar, who, like so many of us, wants answers. Until there are answers Alejandro will remain one of those tragic stories: lost, missing, body never found. Rosy will never have a body to grieve over. And his family will find no peace. No closure. No justice.

Music continues to play in the background. I stop to listen as my all-time favorite Latino singer, Roberto Carlos, sings *La Montaña*. He sings of seeing the light in the darkness, of praying, and keeping faith intact.

The words comfort me a bit, as I struggle to make sense of so many theories, so many possibilities...and as I struggle to have faith that Alejandro is in a good place—somewhere.

Like most mysteries, this is a puzzle with disparate pieces. "I wish I knew what happened for sure, Cesar, but I don't. I wish I could make your heart heal."

We sit in silence until Cesar says, "I'll never understand why he didn't text me, or my mom, or the port captain. Just Luisa, the new girlfriend that we didn't meet until after his disappearance."

He struggles to not cry. "He was out there alone, waiting. You would think he would have. Yet, there were only a few texts. One sent with a picture of him earlier in the day near the big white rock. Then the picture showing the shaded area he supposedly set up, and a couple of messages between him and Luisa, the last one at 2:30 that afternoon. Then nothing."

I ponder his theory, but it doesn't make sense. The texts to Luisa were sent after the picture of the shade material. I take Cesar's hands in mine. "Sweetie, I don't know about the picture without him in it, but the only logical reason I can think of for his not alerting you, your mom, or your sister is lack of cell service. I've been out sailing many times. There are places way out there without service. That's the only reason he wouldn't have contacted you if he was in trouble.

"Or...maybe he just figured they'd be back for him soon enough and he hadn't panicked," I add, "...until they didn't return."

I want to cry. Words from a Paula Hawkins novel I read recently flood my mind. "There can be no greater agony, nothing can be more painful than the not knowing—and that not knowing will never end."

❧ TWELVE ❧

Salvador and I meet for lunch at a taco stand in our neighborhood a few days after Cesar's visit. We sit outside near the street and wave frequently to friends as they walk, bike, or drive by.

"I've collected numerous theories about Alejandro that I want to go over with you," I tell him. "Only a couple of them explain the anonymous phone call telling you to back off."

He brushes hair out of his eyes and, with a big smile and wave, signals the waitress for another beer. "What are they?"

"If Carmen is correct and Alejandro took off on his own, then maybe he had somebody call you and tell you to stop investigating. Or if Martin found him dead and is covering that up, he or somebody else close to him could have placed the call."

"Both are possible," Salvador says with a shrug.

"Or, if the cartel put a hit out on him, either for what happened in Guadalajara or more recently here in La Perlita—maybe they warned you off."

"That's the one I figured from day one, Rebecca. The voice on the phone sounded and felt threatening. I hadn't heard, therefore hadn't considered, your other two possibilities."

"Do you think we called the search effort off too early?" I ask.

Salvador thanks the waitress for the cold Tecate and locks his sad eyes with mine. "No. I think the reason we didn't find him isn't based on the length or breadth of our search, but rather on the lost days before the search started in earnest."

His words make me think back. Alejandro's brother Cesar told Salvador about Alejandro's disappearance on Thursday, shortly after his sister Perla alerted me. Salvador and I spoke by phone soon after, shocked at the news and not sure how to proceed. We agreed to help because the family was desperate, because we all live in the same small neighborhood, and because the pain of our young friend being lost drove us to do something.

I remember thinking, isn't there an established protocol for tragic events like this? Is it really appropriate for a gringa, thousands of miles away, and a small business owner like Salvador to take charge? That would never be the case in the United States.

"Too much wasted time," Salvador says, echoing my own belief. "It took almost two full days for the authorities to move this from 'a tragic accident' to something they needed to investigate more fully."

"What's missing is some type of public alert system, Salvador. In the small California town where I was raised, the fire station alarm goes off at times of emergency and all the volunteers show up to help as needed."

"I agree. Even though a few boats were out looking on Tuesday and Wednesday, the big push didn't take place until Thursday. Just think of all that wasted time!"

Salvador and I reminisce about how we had started with such hope. From my computer, I had disseminated hour-by-hour strategic information on who was searching, which areas were being searched, and where teams were still needed. I posted pictures of the searchers, including a young woman flying in her parasail and government officials organized into groups. Hundreds of locals walked the beaches, volunteers were out in boats and kayaks, and others used ATVs to search. Alejandro's mother cooked and fed volunteers from a friend's house on the beach.

"I thought we would find him alive," I say after taking a sip of my lemonade. "Washed up on a beach, or out by the old sunken barge, or in the crevices of rocks you and others searched by kayak."

We both sit quietly. I let my memories take hold— memories that now hold grief.

I can still feel the hole in my heart and the devastation I had felt as darkness arrived day after day, with no sign of Alejandro. I stew in the what-ifs. What if a full search had begun on Monday afternoon? What if hundreds of boats had flooded the ocean that Tuesday morning looking for Alejandro? What if we'd had money to hire a plane to search on Wednesday morning, rather than having to wait until Friday? What if—

"The timing just sucks," Salvador says, yanking me out of my thoughts. "I was so frustrated when the strong winds stopped the seaplane from taking off on Thursday. It was one more day of so many days...lost. Alejandro out there, alone. We lost against time, Rebecca."

"What do I do now?" I ask my friend. "Just let it go?"

"I think you have to. You're going in circles. Most of these theories have been swirling in this village since day one. If he's alive, maybe one day he'll walk into La Perlita and knock on his mother's front door. If he's dead...well, if he's dead and hasn't floated to some shore somewhere up or down the coast by now, he's probably not going to."

I listen to Salvador's rationale, this friend whom I love and respect. But I can't let go yet. I'm not ready to give up. "I want to talk with Sergio. If he doesn't have anything new, I'll be out of ideas—unless Beto or Lalo will talk to me."

Salvador signals for the check. "They're being tight-lipped. You and I won't get near them, but maybe Sergio can break through. Let me know what you find. By the way, I ran into Captain Ricardo in town a few days ago. He says you ask questions like an interrogator."

I nod and chuckle. "Yep, things did get a bit heated in his office."

A sly smile covers Salvador's face. "Well, he also asked if you're single."

Amusement mixed with excitement fill me. "Really?"

❧ THIRTEEN ❧

"Are you done with your investigation?" Estela asks the following Wednesday, the day before Thanksgiving.

"Almost," I say, setting my beach bag next to me on the sand. "I haven't been able to sit down with Sergio yet. Every time I go to the docks, he's either out fishing or somewhere else. I've left two messages. He hasn't answered my calls."

Patty leans forward. "Is he ignoring you?"

"If he is, there must be a reason," Joanne says, adjusting her sequined sunglasses.

"Why do you have on somebody else's sunglasses?" I tease, avoiding the elephant in the room—*is Sergio avoiding me?*

"These aren't somebody else's glasses. They're my new ones," she says turning her head side to side to give us a full view.

"So why is DKNY engraved on the side? Those aren't your initials."

Patty, Joanne, and Estela chuckle.

"DKNY means Donna Karan New York. These are designer glasses, *amiga.*"

"I'm joking," I say and laugh. "It just made me remember years ago, I went out sailing with this really rich lady. She had on sunglasses like yours and I seriously didn't know why the initials were there. When I asked and she told me…well, I felt a bit foolish, especially because I was wearing a ten-dollar pair."

Joanne's smile broadens. "That is funny. I can't imagine you were ever that naïve, Rebecca."

"Well, I was," I say with a big smile, remembering my country beginnings in a vineyard community.

Estela straightens in her chair and leans forward. "Is it that you don't *want* to delve into why Sergio hasn't called you?" she asks.

"Maybe. A little. Truth is I don't know why. I've left text messages and been to the docks."

I spend a few minutes catching them up on the investigation, explaining Cesar's heart-wrenching visit and Salvador's advice to step away.

"So, what are you going to do?" Patty asks, concern on her pixie face.

"Talk to Sergio and then decide."

We stop chatting for a moment while Luis delivers our margaritas and winks at Joanne.

"Joanne!" we say in unison when he walks away.

"What?" she asks with a big grin.

Estela shakes her head. "Back on topic, ladies. What do you think Sergio might tell you that's any different than what you already know?"

I pause and put my thoughts in order. "He and his father, Efren, have been part of the fishing community for decades. He's respected and hears things we mere mortals may not. I'm hoping he knows Martin's version or has spoken to that second fisherman, Lalo."

Using a napkin, I wipe the wet spot left on the table by my margarita glass and then continue. "If a boat was brought into port under cover of darkness, he may know about that, too. He's the eyes and ears I can't be. Does that make sense?"

"It does to me," Estela says. "You're right, he and his father are like the La Perlita Mafia Dons...but in a good way."

I ask Estela if her Uncle Gil, a fisherman, has shared any pertinent information with her.

"Only that Botas, Captain Martin, and Lalo are all sticking to the same story. As are the two fishermen who helped them pull in the long-line," she says.

"What are the names of the two from the rescuing *panga*?" Joanne asks.

"Alfonso and Beto," Estela and I say at the same time.

I look around and lower my voice. "I expect somebody, the police or the port captain, interviewed them in an official capacity back in June. They were *there*. They could corroborate or refute Captain Martin's story."

Estela interrupts me. "That's what I'm saying. They *are* agreeing with Captain Martin."

"Then maybe they were paid to," I say, sadness filling my heart. "Something bad happened that day and one of those four people have to know what it was!"

We look at each other and shake our heads. I feel hopeless and I don't like the feeling. I want answers.

A bit later, the sun begins to set, and we go through the weekly ritual of settling in, placing our sunglasses on the table, and waiting for the green sunset flash.

"Well?" I ask after the sun has disappeared beyond the horizon.

"I saw it!" Patty says and then adds, "Just kidding."

"I have an idea I want to share," I say a while later, after we have commiserated with Joanne about the breakup with Manuel, her young Latin lover—and cautioned her about her flirtation with Luis.

"What?" they ask.

"It's called 'Alerta/911.' An alert system for La Perlita, so that whenever boaters go missing, an alert is sounded immediately. During my lunch with Salvador the other day, I was telling him how my small hometown responds to emergencies. We need something like that here."

"Do you mean like sounding the tsunami siren?" Estela asks.

"No. Something more high tech. Using cell phones. With an app. Like WhatsApp." I explain my alert system idea and the gals love the concept.

"So, what are your plans?" Joanne asks.

"I'm thinking I need another long visit with Captain Ricardo," I say and smile.

Joanne claps her hands. "Great idea!"

"Why don't you explain it to him over dinner?" Estela suggests, adding air quotes around the word dinner.

"Nah...that would be too forward. By the way, he asked Salvador if I'm single."

"Really?" Joanne sits up straight, beams, and signals Luis for another round of drinks.

❧ FOURTEEN ❧

The next morning, I pop into the Port Captaincy. It's Thanksgiving, but that's not a holiday celebrated in Mexico. "*Buenos dias*, Francisco. Is Captain Ricardo in yet?"

"*Buenos dias*, Rebecca. *Sí.* Let me see if he's available."

After a quick phone call to the back office, Francisco leads me down the hall, knocks on the captain's door, and then motions me forward.

"Rebecca. *Buenos dias.*" Captain Ricardo comes around the desk and gives me a warm hug.

"Thank you for seeing me without an appointment," I say, taking the offered seat, still tingling from his embrace.

After a few moments of small talk, I jump in with an introduction to my newest idea. "You asked me one day why I want to know what happened to Alejandro, and I told you in part because I don't want somebody else to go missing at sea."

"I remember that," he says. "And by the way, I've had this post in La Perlita for five years—I was in Mazatlán before being assigned here. Alejandro's is the first case of a fisherman being lost in that time period. That, of course, doesn't count those two gas runners who purposely drove into the storm."

"Ah, that's why I never ran into you over the last forty-some years I've been coming to La Perlita."

Captain Ricardo sits back in his chair, crosses one leg over the other, and gives me a big smile. "You've been coming here for forty years? You must have been only five when you visited the first time."

"Flattery will get you everywhere," I say, blushing. "But let me tell you why I came to see you today. Back in June, when we called off the search for Alejandro, I posted a promise to the community on my Facebook page that when I returned this season, I would find a way to set up an alert system."

Captain Ricardo listens politely as I share my idea of importing phone numbers into a WhatsApp chat group and then, via one text message, alerting everybody in that circle when a sea-related emergency occurs. "Would you be willing to authorize this and administer the alert?"

"I like your idea and will help you. But I prefer you administer it. Obviously, you're reliable and it's one less thing for me to worry about."

"That works. The good thing about online communications is that I'll have access wherever I am."

We spend the next half-hour discussing, finding, and importing numbers into the Alerta/911 group, including the port captain and his assistant, the naval commander, police chief, and ten other high-profile individuals.

"Anybody else?" I ask, reviewing the contact list.

"That should do it. I expect everyone on this list will be happy to be included, and if not, they'll just opt out."

I close my notebook and smile at the captain. "I'll send out an explanation, along with the invite, as to why we're creating this—and that I have your authorization."

"Any other questions?"

"Yes," I say, with a slight smile. "I want to talk about boat safety."

Captain Ricardo sits back in his leather chair, almost tipping it over, and lets out a full laugh.

I join in.

"Does your mind ever rest, Rebecca?"

"Sometimes, when I'm asleep."

The captain leans forward and writes "boat safety" on a pad of paper. "That is an important subject that will take more time than I have today. How about we meet for dinner early next week?"

My heart does a quick pitter-patter and I'm afraid the heat I feel in my neck will soon be visible on my cheeks. I hide my flushed face by looking down into my bag as I retrieve my notebook. "I would like that. Just not on a Wednesday."

We compare our calendars and choose Tuesday at Sea Master, a restaurant on the beach. I mark it in my notebook and jot down a reminder to see *Señora* Doria for a manicure and pedicure before then.

Another thought comes to mind as I put the notebook away. "By the way, I want to talk to Sergio, and I can't seem to track him down."

"Sergio from the sport fishing association?"

"*Sí.* That Sergio."

"He left about a week ago, motoring down the coast to the port of Barra de Navidad. His parents moved there recently."

"He's not answering my text messages," I say.

"You might have his old number." Captain Ricardo scrolls through his contacts and scribbles on the back of his business card. "Here's the new one."

"*Gracias*, Ricardo." I'm happy to hear Sergio wasn't ignoring me.

"Why are you trying to contact him?"

"More questions about Alejandro."

"You haven't given up yet?"

"Nope." I stand, ready to leave. "See you Tuesday at sunset."

Before hopping on my bike to pedal home, I import Sergio's new number into my phone, add him to the new alert chat group, and text him—hoping he responds.

❧ FIFTEEN ❧

It's Thursday afternoon and I have nothing on my calendar until early evening, when I'll go to a friend's house for Thanksgiving. Back home, I put black beans in the Crockpot to simmer, adding onions, cilantro, garlic, and peppers—my contribution to dinner.

Sitting under an umbrella by the swimming pool downstairs, I open La Perlita's Community Facebook page and let the 2,000 followers know about the new alert system and encourage them to share the information.

A ding on my phone announces a text message from Sergio. He'll be back in La Perlita in a week. I ask him to text or call when he returns.

A week. I have seven days to wait before I talk to Sergio and maybe get more info. That's a long time. I scroll through my list of contacts until I find the municipal chief of police and send him a text.

Comandante Mario. ¿Como estás?

We text back and forth for a few moments and I then ask for a meeting. He tells me he can see me at the coffee shop by the church on Tuesday at 10 a.m.

I check my calendar and smile—coffee with the *comandante* and dinner with the *capitán* all on the same day. That works for me!

Gracias, I text back. See you then.

I've known Mario, the police chief, since he took over the position several years ago. There had been a rash of burglaries in town and I had helped organize a community meeting. The police chief had come to address our concerns.

Tall, with a chiseled body and captivating green eyes, he makes me wish I were twenty-five years younger. I look forward to seeing him and asking questions about the Alejandro investigation. Even though he is responsible for managing a hundred and twenty police officers in this municipality of 36,000 residents—swelling to over 42,000 during the tourist season—he always makes himself available when I call.

It's been nearly a month, and I still have no definitive answer on Alejandro's fate. I had naively thought I'd have some resolution by now. The more dead ends I walk down, the more discouraged I become. I see possibilities in all the theories but am leaning toward a hit from the cartel. Either from whatever it was Alejandro was involved in as a teen in Guadalajara, or because of his actions in La Perlita. I hate the thought, but it is a strong possibility.

I know how scary, violent, and evil the cartel can be when taking over new territory or retaliating against the *federales* or municipal police force. It's a reality and I'm not blind to it. But I'm not afraid of the *local* cartel. I lived next door to and became friendly with a cartel leader and his family some years ago. I learned that if you stay out of their business, they don't mess in yours.

Okay, to be honest, I'm on guard and a little apprehensive about cartel activity, but not shaking-in-my-boots scared...because in our small village, the cartel leaders are financially invested in the community. It's important for them that the tourists wintering in La Perlita feel safe, have a great time, and spend money.

The *comandante,* according to people I know, has a window into the local mafia, which may help me open or close the possibility of cartel involvement in Alejandro's disappearance.

An eighteen-inch greenish-brown iguana creeps along the top of the courtyard wall a few feet from my spot on the lounge chair. I look up and watch him watch me. He turns his head right and left, his dark beady eyes staring me down. He gives me a few push-ups and then lays quiet. I'm not afraid of iguanas, although I am a bit apprehensive because they can be unpredictable. I don't want one of them jumping off the wall toward me. If I stay quiet, he'll finish basking in the afternoon sun and then move on, back into the drainage pipe behind the *casita* in my yard.

I stand up, adjust my bathing suit and walk across the lawn to the pool.

Startled, the iguana scurries away. I say a quick prayer that a neighbor doesn't shoot him with a slingshot and serve him with rice and vegetables for dinner.

❧ SIXTEEN ❧

Rain hammered La Perlita last night, settled the dust on the dirt roads by my house, watered coconut groves, and left puddles big and small before moving on. The online weather page shows the wind will increase throughout the day and the temperature will drop from 92° to 78°.

I wipe the water off a chair on my balcony and settle in with a cup of coffee to enjoy the cool morning and sunrise. Within moments, my house phone rings.

"Rebecca?" a woman asks.

"*Sí.*"

"*Soy* Lorena." I hear the panic in her voice.

"Good morning. *¿Qué pasa?*"

"It's my husband. He didn't come home from fishing last night, and he's still not back!"

"Oh, my gosh, Lorena. Who's the boat captain?" *If it's Captain Martin again, I'll go ballistic.*

"He's our neighbor, Leo. Raul doesn't have any experience. It was his first day out."

I look at my phone. It's seven o'clock. "Get down to the port captain's office right away. Give him full names of the crew and whatever else you know about where they went fishing."

"*Está bien.*"

"How many others are in the *panga*?"

"*Dos*. Leo and Jonaton."

"Okay. I'll send out a message on the 911 chat group."

"*Gracias,* Rebecca. Please pray."

"I will."

Grabbing my cell phone, I open the app and type in, "Alerta. Alerta. Three fishermen have gone missing."

Captain Ricardo responds. "Meet in my office at nine."

"*¡Sí!*"

Other responses come in. "*Enterado.*" I am heartened to see the acknowledgment of the alert.

Lorena and her family live a few streets away from me. I met her several years ago when she asked me to buy diapers for her wheelchair-bound daughter. Not only did I provide diapers, I later treated Lina to lunch at the *Paraiso* restaurant on her eighteenth birthday, and my friend, Captain Dave, invited Lina and her family to a day of sailing with us on his boat. Lina's father is now in danger.

"Please, Lord," I pray as I hurry downstairs to get dressed. "Protect the fishermen. Let us find them. Please let this alert system work to bring them home—for Alejandro's sake."

Two hours later, I park my bike and walk into the Port Captaincy office. Lorena and two other women are already in the room, looking haggard as if they hadn't slept last night.

"*Mucho gusto,*" I say, as Lorena introduces me to the women. Doña Betty, a heavy-set, gray-haired woman, is Captain Leo's wife, and Sara, a young woman probably in her twenties, is recently married to the third fisherman, Jonaton.

"*Buenos días,* Rebecca."

I turn to find my neighbor, Santiago, entering the room. "Santi? *Hola.* Why are you here?"

"It was my *panga* Captain Leo leased."

His response surprises me. I knew he was a fisherman but had no idea he also leased boats.

The men's wives settle into chairs placed in front of Captain Ricardo's desk and Santi follows suit. They fill the small office. The captain gestures for me to sit in his chair while he perches on the left edge of his desk, giving me a good view of the room.

Before the captain launches in with his report, Director Juan Rivas, from the Municipal Civil Protection department, and David Ramos, La Perlita's political representative, walk in and stand by the door. My heart swells with gratitude to see municipal authorities in attendance.

Captain Ricardo informs us he and Francisco have already taken written reports from the wives and from Santi. "The three men left to fish at 1:30 a.m. yesterday morning and were due back in port before nightfall last evening. Shortly after Rebecca activated the alert, two vessels from La Perlita left to search, along with two boats from the port of Sayulita, and two from Punta Mita," Ricardo says in a take-charge voice. "They will be searching thirty miles of coastline, north and south from their specific ports, as well as twenty miles out into the ocean."

He informs us the missing men are apparently not in cell phone range—therefore, no one can track their location. Computer models based on recent sea conditions indicate a strong current is moving north, up the Nayarit coastline.

"Rebecca, we need to get a seaplane ready to fly," the captain says. "I've already called the airport. The cost is 3,500 pesos per hour. We need a minimum of four hours."

All eyes turn to me knowing I've already been through this once with Alejandro's disappearance and have a rapport with the foreign and local community to raise funds. "That's a total of $750.00 U.S.," I say. "We raised more than that for Alejandro when the rescue boats came back empty. Let's make it happen. I still have the bank account we used to receive donations for Alejandro's search. I'll upload the information to my Facebook page and the La Perlita community page."

Mr. Ramos speaks up. "On behalf of the municipal government, we will commit to paying one hour of flight time."

Santi commits to an hour and Lorena, after consulting with the two other wives, agrees to fund an additional hour.

"*Muy bien*," I say. "I'm sure the local and foreign community here in La Perlita will pull together and donate the balance. I'll cover whatever amount is not raised. The important thing is to get the plane in the air as soon as possible."

My heart is racing, and tears threaten to fall when I see the anguished faces of three women who don't know if their husbands will return.

I check my emotions, look at the authorities in the room and ask, "Why don't the *pangas* here in La Perlita have GPS systems?"

Santi responds. "All my boats have portable GPS units."

"So, why is there no signal?"

Lorena responds first. "Because they didn't take the unit with them."

I can't believe what I'm hearing. Especially after Alejandro's tragedy nearly six months ago. "Why not?"

Captain Ricardo turns in my direction. "According to Doña Betty, her husband left the GPS unit at a friend's house and it somehow got ruined. He didn't have time to get it replaced."

Doña Betty's face reddens, and I wonder if it's guilt, remorse, or embarrassment that she's feeling—knowing her husband's lapse in judgment has put his crew at risk.

"*Ay Dios mio!*" I want to shout. How can these boat captains go out into the ocean so unprepared?

"I'll stop by your house in an hour with the 3,500 pesos, Rebecca," Santi says, standing to leave.

David Ramos lets me know he will be by at noon and Lorena, after conferring with her friends, tells me she'll see me around two o'clock. "I don't think we can get the money together before then," she says with sadness.

"That's okay, the pilot needs time to get access to a plane and get it ready to fly. And I need time to get donations in from the Facebook community."

Lorena and the others begin leaving the captain's office. "*Gracias*, everybody," I say, shaking the men's hands and hugging the women.

"Thank you for such quick action, Ricardo," I tell him after everybody has left. "Let's hope it pays off. This is exactly why I want to talk about boat safety. I think you feel the same way I do—these fishermen need to take the ocean more seriously."

The captain acknowledges my statement and then shrugs his shoulders. "I know it's infuriating. They have a saying, '*Se hará la voluntad de Dios.*'"

"Yes, God's will be done. I agree. But they need to do their part." I close my notebook and gather my things. "I'll go home and publicize this online while you contact the pilot. Are there available resources if any additional people want to join the search from here?"

"*Si*. Any boat owner who wants to help can come in and get a fuel voucher."

"*Gracias.* I'll let the community know."

Captain Ricardo escorts me to the door. "*Gracias a ti*, Rebecca. I didn't think we'd need to use the Alerta so soon. Thank God it was ready when we needed it."

It takes me five minutes to pedal my bike back to my neighborhood. I park at my friend Mary's restaurant a block from my house. After filling Mary and her husband Fernando in on the missing fishermen, I order *huevos rancheros* and refried beans for breakfast and then pull up Facebook on my phone.

"Three local fishermen were due home from fishing last night and haven't returned," I write on the small screen. "Searchers are out looking for them. We want to get a seaplane in the air. If you can help, please let me know." With the post, I add the bank card number for donations—the same one we used for Alejandro.

By the time my breakfast is placed in front of me, responses are flowing in from the foreign and local community: "How can this be happening again?" "Why doesn't La Perlita have boat safety?" "How can we help?" "What can we do as a community to stop this from happening?" and, "I'm not in Mexico now; how do I send money?"

I compile a list of individuals willing to work on safety issues, and I provide several ways for people to donate— be it pesos or dollars.

As I finish the meal, my cell phone dings. I read a message within the Alerta chat group from the State Director of Civil Protection advising that the Mexican navy is out looking for the lost fishermen. Within moments the port captain advises us that the one available seaplane and pilot won't be ready until tomorrow morning.

"They'll search by boat today and seaplane tomorrow," I tell Mary and Fernando. "I wish this quick help had been there for Alejandro."

After a restless night worrying about the men lost at sea, I walk upstairs for coffee and call Captain Ricardo's personal phone number, which he'd given me yesterday. The sun is rising behind palm trees in the east, painting the sky in hues of orange and red. Coffee in hand, I settle into a chair on my balcony. I hope the captain is awake.

"*Buenos dias.* Any news?" I ask.

"None. Crews searched yesterday until dark. They're probably back out this morning. I just got into the office to start monitoring the activity. How's the fundraising going?"

I set my cup on the side table. "Great. I have the money. Let's get the plane in the air. How do I pay the pilot?"

"Hold on. Let me call him from my office phone."

A few moments later, the captain comes back on the line. "We need to hold off on the air search today. There's a strong westerly wind off the coast from the recent storm. It could take down the small plane. We can't risk that."

I take a deep breath and want to scream. *Déjà* vu echoes in my brain. The same thing happened with Alejandro! "What do we do?"

"We continue using the boats and manpower to search along the coast until the wind subsides. Francisco and I will go out about ten o'clock."

I agree to update the community and keep watch on the Alerta/911 circle. "Please, Lord," I pray. "Watch over Raul, Leo, and Jonaton. It's been two cold nights. Keep them safe."

From my balcony, I see Pepe, the neighborhood goat boy, with fifty or more of his herd. He encourages them forward with a long stick as he follows behind on his horse. Their bleating is comforting, a reminder of why I love living here in rural Mexico. I remain on guard, however, to be sure Pepe doesn't let the goats stop and munch on the dozen red bougainvillea I've planted on the street side of my privacy wall.

"*Buenos dias*," I call down.

"*Buenos dias, Señora.*"

"*Gracias por cuidarme las plantas*," I say giving him two thumbs up.

"*De nada*," he responds, and prods the animals on past my place and out into the empty lot on the corner.

Hours later, I walk into town over dirt roads and cobblestone streets to meet Lisa for an early dinner. The leisurely fifteen-minute stroll allows me to stop along the way to say *hola* and chat with friends also walking or biking into town. The wind is blowing, and I give up trying to keep my hair in place. It seems everybody has heard about the missing fishermen, and they ask if there's any word.

"No," I reply sadly. "Keep praying."

I open the front gate and enter the courtyard of the Bungalows—the small hotel my sister Tina and brother-in-law Joaquin built thirty years ago. "Is the plane up and searching?" my niece asks.

"No. It's grounded because of the weather." I look up at the second-story home above the hotel, half-expecting Tina to walk out the front door and call out a "Hello, baby sister" greeting. "Dang, I miss your mom."

"I know. Me, too. I still haven't adjusted to her death."

Lisa and I walk five minutes from the hotel down to Nacho's Restaurant on the beach. We stroll by storefronts jam-packed with white hammocks, hand-painted pottery, brightly colored blouses and dresses, and items painted or engraved with "La Perlita."

Because of today's relentless wind, we ask to sit inside behind the floor-to-ceiling glass window. Lisa orders white wine to be followed by fish and chips and I ask for coconut shrimp and lemonade. I stare out at the ocean, hoping to spot a boat returning to port towing a *panga* with three happy fishermen.

Nothing.

"This not knowing is killing me," I say. "It reopens the Alejandro wound."

"I know. I think we all feel that way. Let's hope the quick organization for search-and-rescue makes a difference this time."

The late afternoon passes as we enjoy our meal, and later greet and visit with friends coming into the restaurant for sunset and dinner. When the sun begins to touch the horizon, we order margaritas and wait, cozy at our table by the big window.

I keep glancing at my phone for an alert, but there's no news. *Panga* after *panga* returns from a full day of fishing, and search-and-rescue boats come back empty-handed.

This will be the third night the fishermen are out in the elements, presumably adrift.

Signaling for our check, I gather my belongings and drape a shawl over my shoulders. As I'm putting the phone in my bag, I hear a "ding." Hands shaking, I grab the phone and check WhatsApp. Nothing. But there's a voice message from Lorena. Please, Lord, let it be good news.

"Rebecca—Raul and the other two men are alive! They're on their way into port. I'll text you later with more info."

"Hold on, Lisa!" I shout, seeing my niece head through the front door. "The fishermen are alive!"

Lisa, friends, and restaurant staff erupt into applause.

With a huge smile and a grateful heart, I text the message into the Alert system, "The fishermen have been found!"

"Great news" and "Thank the Lord" messages flood back into the chat group.

Captain Ricardo informs us he's heading to the docks to wait for the men. He asks Juan Rivas, the civil protection director, to order an ambulance and paramedics to meet him there.

"Who found them?" I ask.

"Three guys in a *panga* on their way back in for the day spotted them offshore near a mangrove."

I immediately post to Facebook, "Thank you, everybody. The fishermen are safe. We don't need the seaplane. If you donated today and have your receipt showing the donation, please contact me for a refund. Hugs."

Back home thirty minutes later, the house phone rings. "Rebecca? *Soy Lorena.*"

"*Buenas noches, Lorena. Digame.* How's Raul?"

"He's fine. They're all cold, tired, and hungry. But very grateful. The paramedics checked them out. They're good."

She tells me the captain and crew had a boat full of fish and were ready to return to port when the motor failed. The current and waves moved them around and they drifted for three days.

"They must have been scared," I say.

"Raul was terrified. But the captain kept them safe. He says they used the melted ice in the coolers for drinking and cut up fish to soak in the salty sea water to eat like *ceviche*."

"That was smart," I say, wishing Alejandro had been trained in ocean survival.

She tells me they tried to use their weight to rock and maneuver the boat and get close to shore, but that didn't work. Especially when the wind broadsided them.

"A small fishing crew found them?"

"*Si*. Three men heading back into port. Raul says they saw the searchers looking for them yesterday. They stood, waved, and shouted, but weren't seen. They could tell the guys on those boats were looking away from the shore and missed them."

"Oh, my gosh, Lorena. That must have been devastating. Help so near, but not near enough."

"Raul says he got really emotional and thought they were going to disappear...like Alejandro did."

My heart breaks and my frustration mounts. If the fishermen would leave port with a small backpack of essentials, like a GPS system, flares, or a mirror—something to signal other boats—the chances of rescue would be much greater.

"Then this evening," Lorena continues, emotion in her voice, "they were just getting ready to lie down for another night of sleep when they saw a small crew of fishermen looking their way. They jumped up and down and were seen!"

The joy in her voice is contagious. Smiles of gratitude fill my face. Happy tears fall.

❧ SEVENTEEN ❧

It's Tuesday morning. I awake, stretch and search my memory for what's on my schedule. It takes but a moment for the brain cells to fire. Coffee with *Comandante* Mario at ten this morning, and dinner tonight with Captain Ricardo. How lucky am I to sit across the table from two handsome men on the same day.

I sing a happy song in the shower. The three missing fishermen have been home with their families for two days now and I'm sure they're also waking up happy. *If only Alejandro had been found.*

I start my morning walk into town. The potpourri of scenes fill me like spices in my favorite food. A young man atop a horse trots by, texting on his phone. I chuckle. Really? Two dozen day workers, crammed into the back of a small, dilapidated pickup truck, rumble by on their way to work in construction or the chili fields. A family of four, including a baby, pass by on a motorcycle. I shake my head and cringe. I know it is illegal to have so many people on a motorcycle, but it happens every day—out of necessity when families can't afford a more suitable vehicle. Adults and children have been killed in motorcycle accidents in and around this village and those not killed have lost limbs. I say a prayer for this family as they zoom by.

Just before ten o'clock, I enter the French bakery across the street from the Catholic Church and select an outside table for two. My spot is behind a planted fern with large fronds that will partially shield me from those passing on their way down Beach Street. While waiting for the police chief, I check the mirror one last time to make sure my curls are in place.

"*Comandante!*" I say with a big grin as Mario approaches moments later. I admire his uniform, which is all black with a holster and gun on his hip. His big black boots give him an additional inch of height on me.

"*Buenos dias*, Rebecca," he says, his green eyes smiling.

We share a hug and sit. "How have you been?" I ask.

"*Bien.*"

I ask what's new in the police world. He smiles but gives me no insight into the local world of crime, although he does check his phone when a new message comes in.

"*Buenos dias, Rebecca. Buenos dias, Comandante,*" Marisol, the bakery owner, says, ready with her order pad and pencil.

"Coffee and a blackberry croissant," I say.

Mario orders the same and asks for separate checks.

Hmmm. I guess that must be police procedure.

After our coffee arrives, I blurt out my question. "Did Alejandro Garcia disappear because of a cartel hit?"

The police commander laughs and sits back in his chair. "You don't mess around, do you?"

"I know you're a busy man," I say, with a coy smile. "And I really want to figure out this mystery. It just doesn't make sense. We recently had three fishermen go missing in a disabled *panga* and *they* were found. But not Alejandro."

"Did you know the young man?"

"Yes. And his family. I can't say I know everything he ever did, nor *all* the details of what was happening in his life when he disappeared. But he doesn't fit the profile in my mind of someone who should have been targeted by a *sicario* of the cartel."

The *comandante* raises an eyebrow as I use the Spanish word *sicario* for hitman or assassin. Probably not a word most foreigners would have come to know, but then, I'm not your average foreigner. "I've heard the rumor of him dating a cartel member's girlfriend," I say. "Is that a sin subject to death?"

Mario's face turns serious. We stop talking for a moment while Marisol sets warm croissants on the table and leaves. He leans forward. "There's a lot about the cartel and their actions that defy common sense," he says, lowering his voice. "Is that a reason to be killed? Not in normal society. But in the mafia world...sure. Especially if you grasp the fact that the majority of cartel members are high on drugs most of the time and drink liquor like water. They've been known to kill for the slightest offense, or just for the thrill, or on a dare."

I dip a piece of croissant into my coffee and stare at the police chief. "I've heard that, but don't want it to be true, especially locally."

"I understand you don't want it to be true, Rebecca, but that doesn't change reality. The local *plaza* leader and his crew are ruthless. Do you know what a *plaza* leader is?"

"I do. A *plaza* is a selling zone. And the *plaza* leader does everything possible, good or bad, to keep his territory intact. I learned that from my neighbor, Toro, who ruled this area years ago before you became chief of police."

"Yes, that was before my time. But I've heard about him. The difference between your neighbor and the current plaza leader is that, from what I've been told, Toro was raised here in La Perlita and had a heart for the people. He would discipline, but not necessarily kill every rival. The new guy, put here by the Jalisco Cartel, doesn't care who you are. A drug user will be severely punished for just buying from a rival. The leader's logo is stamped on the paper used to wrap a joint. If you're caught smoking a joint without that logo you can be beaten, almost to death. The person who sold you the pot—or meth or cocaine—will be killed."

Although what he is telling me is not new, I still squirm in my chair and my heart hurts with an image of young Alejandro being murdered. "So it is possible that an irrational, drugged cartel member could have killed Alejandro on that *panga* and made the boat and the body disappear?"

"Possibly, yes—if he had the approval of the boat captain and the other fisherman on board. But that wouldn't have stayed quiet among the cartel members. If it had happened, I would have heard about it not long after."

"Can you tell me why you're so sure?"

"No."

I don't want to press him, so I prepare to change the subject. Before I can ask my next question, Mario's phone rings. He looks at the caller ID, stands, and mouths, "*Un momento*," before he moves to the corner of the patio. With his back turned to me he answers the call. I hope he isn't going to leave.

Moments later, he returns, sits down, and finishes his coffee. "I've been called away," he says, taking a fifty-peso bill from his wallet.

"I understand. But before you go—can you just tell me if there is anything you have heard or learned that tells you Alejandro was killed by someone? Anyone?"

"All indications are that he wasn't. Something happened that day—and it is suspicious—but there's no evidence it points to any cartel or person. The police investigators looked into the cartel's and the boat captain's involvement as part of their investigation. And think about it. If they wanted him dead…why not just kill him on land?"

"Hmmm. That's true. Killing him on land would have been easier. Is the investigation ongoing?"

"It's open but not active. There's been no new information that brings it to the top of the list of disappearances being investigated."

"How many are on that list?" I ask.

"I'm not at liberty to give you numbers for this municipality. But it's public knowledge that some five thousand people have disappeared in the state of Jalisco over the last four years."

"That many? Dang!"

"That's only Jalisco," he says. "Thirty-six percent are between 16 and 28 years old. And it's almost all about seizing plazas or gaining control of principal drug trafficking routes."

"And you're sure Alejandro isn't one of that number?"
"Yes."

Again, I want to ask how he can be so sure and how he knows these things…but I don't.

We stand and hug.

"Thank you, *Comandante* Mario. I'll scratch the 'cartel hit' theory off my list of possible reasons for Alejandro's disappearance."

"You take care, Rebecca. You might want to stop poking around on this subject. It can get you into trouble even absent the cartel angle."

"I'm almost done gathering information. And if I do get into trouble, I'll call you," I say with a big smile, wanting to make light of such distressing news.

The police chief smiles back. "You do that," he says and walks away.

❧ EIGHTEEN ❧

Later that evening, after spending the afternoon planning a community event for January, I stroll into the Sea Master restaurant located beachside, two blocks before the docks. I'm a few minutes late, having agonized over what to wear. Dressy? Not dressy? Casual? Capris and a T-shirt? I am inexplicably nervous about this dinner meeting. That's not like me. I chose cropped white pants with embroidered flowers at the hem, and a peach tank top beneath a sleeveless sheer peach blouse. My white sandals show off yesterday's pedicure.

Abel, the restaurant owner and my dear friend, greets me with a warm hug and kiss.

"The port captain is awaiting you, Rebecca," he says with a sly smile.

"No need to smile that way, Abel," I reply with a grin. "It's just a business meeting."

His smile widens. "Of course. I'm sure that's why you look especially lovely this evening and why Capitan Ricardo looks so handsome in his dress whites."

Keeping his grin in place, Abel takes my arm and escorts me to the outside deck overlooking the ocean. Flowing swatches of white linen crisscross the thatched roof from corner to corner and candles have been placed on the outside tables waiting for dusk. I hadn't consciously considered how romantic this venue could be in the evenings when I chose this restaurant for our "meeting."

"Good evening," Captain Ricardo says, standing to greet me. "How beautiful you look."

I find myself blushing but enjoy the compliment. He holds my chair as I take a seat. He is, in fact, dressed in formal white attire with his impressive emblems secured above his shirt breast pocket. I had noticed in my quick but thorough assessment that even his boots are white.

Abel hands us the wine list and menus. I know from experience my favorite wine, Gewurztraminer, is not on the list, so I order the house Chardonnay. Ricardo orders the house red along with calamari as an appetizer for us to share. He doesn't ask for separate checks. Hmmm.

It's nearing sunset as we toast and sip our wine. I exhale the stress I'd built up just getting to this moment and am grateful the breaking waves hide my audible sigh.

"Do you come here often?" the captain asks, looking around.

"I do. Abel is a good friend and we work together on the town council. So, I'm usually here attending an event meeting. And you?"

"No, I don't go out much at night. Annie and Abby miss me and don't like me out late. They're my babies and I don't want them to be sad."

"Annie and Abby? Oh, yes, your twin poodles. You seem very attached to them." *The dogs! Geez.*

"I am," he says, like a proud daddy. "My ex-wife didn't understand…but they're the best thing that's ever happened to me."

"How nice," I say, hoping to sound sincere. "My ex-boyfriend used to say that same thing about his dog." Déjà vu—all over again. The image of the captain fawning over his dogs compounds my ex-boyfriend-caused PTSD and yells at me to *Run!*

Not saying a word, we both look out at the ocean. He's obviously missing his dogs, I think. I swallow and calm my breathing. *Think sunset. Think sunset.* The mantra works. The lingering sunlight's reflection on the gentle waves turns them metallic blue, which captivates and soothes me.

As we sit in silence, the sun begins to set. "Have you ever seen the 'green flash?'" I ask.

He nods. "*Sí*, I have."

"I haven't," I confess. I relax for a moment enjoying the cool, beautiful evening before we both return our attention to the yellow ball dipping beyond the horizon.

"Watch carefully," Captain Ricardo says.

I take off my sunglasses and stare, and stare, and stare. Just as the sun disappears, I see a thin green line on the horizon where the sun had been. "I saw it," I say, a bit deflated. "But I didn't see a flash. Only a green line that was there for a micro-moment."

"That's it," he says.

"That's it?" I ask. "Dang. I expected more."

We toast to the green line and I silently hope it's not an omen to the outcome of this evening.

Carlos, Sea Master's main waiter, sets the fried calamari on the table and gives me a wink and a conspirator's grin.

"This isn't a date!" I mouth to him from behind my menu.

Standing near my chair, Carlos lights the candle on our table and gives me another big smile. I kick him gently while ordering avocado stuffed with shrimp and Captain Ricardo asks for a ribeye.

"So, about boat safety," I say.

The captain sits back in his chair and adjusts his shirt collar. "Yes, boat safety."

"What laws must be changed to make sure that every boat, regardless of its size, has some type of safety equipment on board—most importantly, life jackets and flares?"

"The law already exists," he says.

I almost choke on my wine. "How can that be?"

"The maritime laws outline what is required on every boat leaving port." By memory, he lists the required gear—a VHS radio, rope, mirror, life vests, GPS unit..."

I stop him. "So why didn't the *panga* Alejandro was on have any of that?"

"Because the fishermen choose not to follow the law. Many say they can't afford the equipment, or they don't want to use space for 'things' which take up room they need for the fish they will catch."

A sea of emotions washes over me—anger, sadness, disbelief. "Whose job is it to make sure the law is followed?"

"Mine."

I'm seething inside but respect his honesty. "So, why aren't you successful in enforcing these regulations?"

He explains that he wants all vessel owners to obey the law, but he can't make them. There are too many boats leaving at all hours, and he doesn't have enough manpower or equipment to supervise them. It's an open port; there is no gate to go through. The sport fishing boats follow the regulations, as do the big commercial fishing companies. "It's the small *pangas* that leave in the middle of the night or early morning hours that are under our radar and most at risk."

Carlos arrives with our food. "*Gracias*. It looks delicious," I say.

"*Provecho*," Ricardo says, preparing to cut into his steak.

"Bon appétit," I respond and take a bite of the delicious avocado and shrimp.

After a few moments, I ask. "What about the naval authority? Don't they spot check? I went fishing last year and we were stopped by a navy vessel. They inspected the boat and reviewed the captain's paperwork."

"They can and do. But it's random. And again, we have long-liners like Captain Martin, who motor out under the cover of darkness."

"Long-line fishing is illegal," I say. "So why haven't you arrested him?"

Captain Ricardo takes another bite of his steak. "It's tasty. Do you want to try it?"

"Thank you, but no. I don't eat red meat unless it's ground into a hamburger or taco."

"Really? You should try this."

I decline nicely and return to my question. "Why haven't you arrested Captain Martin?"

The captain wipes his mouth and sets his napkin next to his plate. "Because I haven't caught him in the act."

I wonder about his lack of eye contact and wonder if this dashing port captain gets his pockets lined to look the other way, like my friend Estela has told me. "If you or the navy patrol had caught him, and taken away his fishing rights, he wouldn't have been out long-lining the day Alejandro disappeared."

"We can't catch them all. The day and time they go out is unpredictable and it's a huge ocean."

I cross my arms and sit up straight. "There has to be a way."

"I've tried everything, Rebecca. There are required inspection days, where I find *all* the boats with the proper equipment onboard. That doesn't mean they'll be equipped the next day, though."

I see the captain's frustration written on his face. It feels real.

Breathing softly, measuring my words, I stop to watch a large fishing boat motoring back into port. The masthead and stern lights shine in the dark. Are they fully equipped? I wonder.

"Do you want help?" I finally ask. "I've met a few retirees in town who have maritime experience in their own countries. They're willing to offer some ideas."

His look is guarded. "What exactly do they want to help with?"

"They have ideas on how to better outfit the *pangas*. They would like to even bring safety equipment in from Canada or the States to get to the poorer fishermen."

"That sounds good, and I'm willing to meet with them, but like I said, the fishermen have everything they legally need. It's a matter of them taking it out with them."

We discuss ways to rally the fishing crews toward safety—including educating school children so they pressure their fathers to be safe.

After dinner, and declining the offer of dessert, Ricardo pays the bill even though I offer to pay my half. "It's been my pleasure, Rebecca."

Away from the direct ocean breeze, it's too warm to use the shawl I brought, so I wrap it around my neck like a scarf and we walk toward the taxi stand. Ricardo reaches over and wraps my arm in his, cupping his hand over mine. I want to feel chemistry but don't.

Pancho, the taxi driver, sees us approaching and opens the back door. "*Buenas noches*, Rebecca. *Buenas noches, Capitán.*"

As we settle in the back seat next to each other, Ricardo takes my hand and caresses it. I again wait for the chemistry to capture me, and feel nothing.

"*Buenas noches*, Pancho. Can you drop the captain off at his house and then take me home?" I ask, wanting to short-circuit any other thought my dinner companion may have.

A surprised look crosses Ricardo's face.

I smile. "Sorry about cutting the evening short, but I have some paperwork I need to finish this evening. Thank you for dinner. I'll get back to you soon about a meeting with the friends I mentioned. And I'll text the middle school director and have her contact you to schedule a general assembly presentation. I'll ask Santi and Raul, Lorena's husband, about joining you for that event. Does that sound alright with you?"

Pancho pulls up in front of the captain's house. "Um, why...sure. *Está bien.*"

"Good night," I say as he pays the driver and walks away.

"Thank the Lord it's Wednesday," I say to nobody in particular the following evening. With purpose in my step, I stride into the Oasis Bar for my weekly get-together with the margarita gals. I have so much to download.

I give Rafa a hug and walk briskly across the tiled floor, down the wooden steps, and onto the sand where

Estela, Joanne, and Patty have all settled in at our table and are ordering drinks.

"*Hola*, Luis," I say before sitting down. "The usual, please."

"Tell us, tell us, tell us!" Patty almost squeals.

Joanne's eyes sparkle. "I was just saying that I saw you with Captain Ricardo last night at Sea Master. The two of you were dressed so elegantly."

"Did you go home with him?" Estela wants to know.

"No!" I say, face in my hands. "The closest I got to his house was when Pancho, the taxi driver, let him off at his front door."

"Why? What happened?" they ask.

"There's no *there* there," I say.

"No *there* there?" Estela asks. "What does that mean?"

"It means I'm not going to start down an intimate road where there's no place to get to. Something about him just doesn't work for me...on a visceral level."

Luis sets our napkins, drinks, and peanuts on the table, smiles at Joanne and leaves to our chorus of "*Gracias!*"

I inhale the first sip of my blended margarita and find myself in the midst of a brain freeze. *Ouch!*

"I don't get it," Joanne says. "I could see the two of you from my table next door at Nacho's. You were basked together in candlelight, and it looked so...perfect."

Several deep breaths warm my freezing brain and I launch in with my concerns and gut feelings. "I wanted it to be—but two major things killed any romantic feelings on my part—starting with my nagging fear that the good captain 'se presta.'"

"Say pressa? What does that mean?" Patty asks.

"*Se presta*," Estela clarifies. "It means for a price he's willing to look the other way."

"I hope that's not true," I say, "but there are many un-answered questions that point to him not doing his job in a timely, thorough manner."

"That's what my uncle and several other fishermen have said," Estela reminds me. "And, I met a port captain from another area of Mexico a few months after Alejandro went missing. He told me military helicopters are at their disposal for accidents at sea. That didn't happen here. Not for Alejandro and not for the three men lost recently."

Her statement makes me want to cry. "I don't get it. How can the port captain not use every means at his dis-posal? Is our village just too small to receive that kind of assistance?"

Estela says that is a possibility.

"I don't want to judge the port captain," I say. "There may be a good reason for every decision he has made. And someday I'll delve deeper into that conversation with him. In the meantime, that's not the only reason I say there's no *there* there."

Patty leans forward and grasps her glass in both hands. "What's the other?"

"His dogs!"

Chuckles erupt around our table, lightening up the mood. "You and dogs," Joanne says. "Are you seriously going to let a man's relationship with his dogs keep you from getting love, affection, and...*sex*?"

I sit back in my chair and cross my arms. "Yes! In my mind, a man is fundamentally needy when he uses an animal to fill an emotional void. It's not normal—in my traumatized opinion, at least."

"Maybe he just cares about them. People do love their dogs, you know," Joanne says.

"There's a difference between loving and caring about dogs and making them human and choosing them above your partner."

Estela reaches over and touches my shoulder. "Wow, your ex really did traumatize you, Rebecca."

"Yes, he did. That's why he's my ex. I'm not walking down that road again."

Joanne raises her glass. "Let's toast to the concept of 'love your pet sensibly.'"

"Amen. And to healthy 'human relations,'" I add with a laugh, wanting to make light of myself and my humanized dog phobia.

❧ NINETEEN ❧

I awake this morning straight out of an Alejandro dream. The weirdness of the dream clings to me like wet clothes.

I saw Alejandro in the *panga*, his skin the darkest shade of brown. I could hear his prayers, still believing people were searching for him. He had hoped to see a boat, helicopter, or plane by now but has not seen or heard anything. He knew he'd be hard to find. The fiberglass boat was small. Even when docked among regular commercial fishing boats, *pangas* escape notice.

But Martin would not give up and lose his fishing boat... would he?

Alejandro spotted a brown paper sack and a plastic water bottle bopping in the water nearby. He leaned precariously over the side of the *panga*, scooped them up, squeezed the water out of the bag, and turned it into a ball. He threw the sack out ahead of the boat and watched the *panga* reach the sack a few minutes later. He was definitely drifting...somewhere.

Desperate to feel in control, he notched his daily mark on the bench seat and looked around to calculate his location. The sun was rising behind him. The sea was his master as the boat continued to move slowly in the opposite direction. *I'm drifting west, or maybe southwest. I just know I'm heading out to sea, caught up in a current.*

Alejandro licked his dry, cracked lips. He barely had enough saliva to wet them. It hadn't rained in two days. His eyes burned. Alone with his thoughts, Alejandro stared at the pale pink and peach colors of the sunrise. Another day burgeoned with its promise of hope. He tried to keep his mind focused on good things—Nando, palm trees, a cold Corona. *I can do this. I will survive.*

An albatross landed on top of the disabled motor. *Can I catch him?* The seabird turned its head to look at Alejandro and then flew away as Alejandro lurched. *Next time.*

He took shelter under the shade material. He thanked God for his family and prayed for his son. He remembered the pain when Nando's mother, his now ex-girlfriend, had moved on in her life, taking Nando and leaving him behind.

"You are the shining joy in my heart, my little *hijo*." He touched the locket still around his neck, now attached with fishing twine. He opened the locket and looked at Nando's sweet face. "Don't cry, my son," he said aloud in a raspy voice. "You will always be with me, as I will be with you, every time you think of me."

Two little poodles, licking the salt from Alejandro's face, jolted me awake.

It takes two cups of strong coffee and cleansing prayer to shake off the top layer of the dream. "Where is he, Lord?" I ask.

I wait, hoping for a still, small voice or a revelation that tells or shows me something.

Nada.

"Please keep him safe, Lord. *Por favor.*"

A while later, I receive a text from Sergio.

I'm in La Perlita. Let's meet this afternoon?
Si. Por favor. 2 de la tarde. At your slip on the docks. ¿Está bien?
Si. Nos vemos.

It's mid-December. The cooler weather is a great indicator we are getting close to winter in La Perlita—I only needed two of my three bedroom fans to keep me cool last night.

I feel conflicted as I get out of the shower to dress and ride my bike into town. Alejandro's been missing for six months and I'm almost at the end of my list searching for answers. I accept the notion he was lost at sea. But was it truly a tragic accident—or was it murder?

I've covered a lot of territory since my plane touched down in Puerto Vallarta, but I have no real answers. Last night's dream remains in my mind. Is Alejandro alive? Was the dream a sign from the Lord? Or was it just my emotions surfacing?

I've researched dreams and learned there are several theories about why they occur: They are a way for us to consolidate and process information gathered during the day; they're a working form of psychotherapy; they represent unconscious desires and wishes. And while all of those theories seem logical, I don't dismiss the good Lord speaking to us through dreams.

Later in the morning, I stop by to visit Mary and Fernando at their restaurant on the corner. I'm craving a bean, egg, ham, and cheese breakfast burrito, served with fresh fruit, avocado slices, and orange juice.

Mary's personal story diverts from the majority of those who migrate to La Perlita from mountain villages in the state of Guerrero, south of Jalisco, to live here and sell their arts and crafts on the beach.

In Mary's case, her mother sent her away from their poor rural community—where formal education was not available—and off to school in the city, six hours away by bus. Mary stayed with and worked for an affluent family. In the process, she got both an education and a husband. Fernando, from a prosperous family, was forced to choose between his girlfriend from an indigenous community and his family. He chose Mary and they moved to La Perlita.

I'm glad they did, because Fernando, Mary, and their three adult children are like family to me. And Mary's always the first one to raise her hand to help me with my community projects.

"I'm meeting with Sergio the fisherman this afternoon," I tell them over breakfast.

"He's a good one to talk to," Fernando says. He leaves for a moment to say goodbye to a table of four customers across the room.

"How's that knee?" I ask, watching him limp back. "Are you finally going to give up playing goalie for the over-the-hill soccer league?"

"We're not *that* old," he says and grimaces.

Mary leaves the kitchen, dries her hands on her apron, and sits next to me. "He won't listen to me," she says, picking up her embroidery. "He'll be back out there again as soon as that knee heals."

We spend a few moments talking about Fernando's love of soccer and the dress she is embroidering for her granddaughter, and then I lament about my lack of progress on finding what happened to Alejandro.

"What about Captain Martin? What does he say?" Mary asks.

"He's been interrogated by the port captain and the police. Apparently, his version hasn't changed—when they returned to where they left the disabled *panga*, Alejandro and the boat were gone. End of story."

Fernando leans forward and places his elbows on the table. "Have you talked to the third fisherman, Lalo, and the others on the rescue boat—Alfonso and Beto?"

"No. I've been told they're not talking to others, so they're definitely not going to talk to an unknown, curious *gringa*. Which is why I'm reaching out to Sergio. If they've said anything, I'm thinking he will have heard."

A few hours later, Sergio greets me at the docks with a chest-crushing bear hug. Standing six feet tall and three feet wide, he reminds me of the comedy actor Larry the Cable Guy.

"It's been too long, Rebecca," he says, giving me a wide, friendly smile that lights up his face.

"I feel the same, although I have come to look for you a few times."

"I heard about that. Sorry. I'm refinishing several charter boats and I had to make a trip south to check on my parents. They're in their eighties now."

We talk a bit about Barra de Navidad, the quaint fishing village three hours south where his parents now live.

"I can imagine what you want to talk about," Sergio says.

I chuckle. "Am I that transparent?"

He offers me a seat on an upside-down metal bucket near his fancy fishing boat. The familiar smells of fish and diesel permeate the air around us. "Nothing stays hidden in this town. What else is there to do but fish, eat, have babies, and gossip?"

His words are pretty accurate. It's amazing how many teenagers walk around town carrying or pushing little ones in strollers. "Babies having babies," is how I think of them. I remember saying those words to Alejandro and Maria when I first saw them with their baby, Nando, two years ago.

"So, what do you know about Alejandro?" I ask.

Sergio retrieves a wooden half-barrel abandoned nearby and places it next to me to use as a chair. "Tell me first what you've found out with all your questioning," he says, once seated.

I count off the seven theories I gathered before and after arriving in La Perlita: 1) Alejandro died in a tragic accident at sea; 2) he faked his own death; 3) he was killed by the cartel for something that happened in Guadalajara years ago; 4) a cartel member killed him for messing around with the guy's girlfriend; 5) the *panga* became a sailboat and the wind took him away to parts unknown; 6) Captain Martin returned to find him drowned and covered up the death so he wouldn't be charged with criminal negligence—

"And number seven," I say finally, "a psychic told Alejandro's mother that he's alive but he doesn't know where."

"Interesting. And which one do you believe?"

I stare out into the lagoon and organize my thoughts. Turning back to him, I say, "I find them all plausible. But there's no evidence for any of them. The more I hear, the more questions I have."

"What are they?" he asks.

"For starters, where's the body and where's the *panga*? Those two are at the top of my list, followed by *who* called Salvador and told him to stop investigating Alejandro's disappearance? And then, why wasn't Captain Martin arrested, put into a cell, and interrogated?"

Sergio crosses his arms and looks at me with a serious expression. "Those are good questions. Tell me about the call Salvador received. I heard a rumor, but no details."

"I thought you knew everything," I say with a chuckle. "And you're acting like a shrink—listening, inquiring, but answering nothing." I tilt my head. "Isn't this when you ask, 'And how does that make you feel?'"

His smile broadens. "How *does* that make you feel?"

"This whole thing sucks, *Doctor* Sergio," I respond, only half teasing.

We share a laugh and I explain how Alejandro's family agreed with Salvador and me to call off our search, but Salvador and Cesar kept asking around about Martin and Lalo. "We were angry they hadn't been arrested for, at least, leaving Alejandro alone in that *panga*."

"You weren't the only ones," he says.

"Well, a few days later, Salvador received the anonymous call to stop his inquiries."

I take the notebook and pen out of my bag. "So. Your turn. What do you think or know? I'm most interested at this point in Captain Martin. What is he saying? What did the other fishermen say who were present that day? Was Alejandro murdered? Did he drown? Those four guys must hold the answer."

Sergio steps down into his boat tied up next to us and retrieves two bottles of water from a cooler. He hands me one.

Sitting side-by-side, we pause in silence for a moment and look out into the freshwater lagoon. Water taxis motor across the vast waterway, taking passengers to and from the restaurants on the Las Brisas side or the golf course fifteen minutes away. People are smiling and happy—the majority being tourists enjoying weeks or months in this paradise.

It's sad that we gaze upon idyllic surroundings while discussing the possible murder of a young man.

"I've been as interested as you are in this tragic event, Rebecca. I was out searching for Alejandro the morning after he was reported missing. I've kept my ears and eyes open. Something feels suspicious, because of what you said—no body, no boat. But I haven't found any answers, which is why I'm interested in your conclusions."

"Or lack of them," I say, frustrated.

"If Martin and his crew are covering up a murder or even Alejandro's accidental death by drowning, they haven't given any sign. It's been over six months. It'd be difficult to keep something like that concealed for so long."

I finish my water and place the bottle inside my bag for later disposal. "I agree. It's logical that at least one of the fishermen would have let something slip during their meetings with the port captain or the police investigators. Right?"

Sergio stretches out his long legs. "Or more likely, one of them would have let something slip during a night of heavy drinking. That's what I mean when I say I've been listening, waiting for a clue to drop."

"You'll need to hang out late at a lot of bars, then," I say. "Good luck with that."

"We local fishermen gather at just a few select places. It's doable. And I have *compadres* on alert, too."

His answer encourages me and reminds me of a Bible verse, "All that is hidden will be revealed." I stand and stuff my notebook back in my bag. "So now what? Sit and wait? I feel like I've failed."

"We all want answers, Rebecca." Sergio rises and embraces me. "I promise to keep on this."

His warm hug and pledge are comforting. "From what I've heard, you've sifted through a lot of sand looking for resolution."

I break the embrace and step away. "Yeah, well, all I've found are crushed seashells." I start to leave, but pause. "One more question. What about the call Salvador received?"

Sergio shrugs. "That's a tough question. It could've been someone from the cartel or just somebody who believes Martin is innocent and wanted Salvador to back off. Hopefully we'll find out some day."

After three months of organizing and leading town events to raise money for local schools—with no breakthroughs on Alejandro's disappearance—my time in La Perlita comes to an end. My niece, Lisa, drives me to the Puerto Vallarta airport at the end of March.

"Are you sad to leave?" she asks as we buckle in.

"Yes and no. I love getting back to the States—anticipating hugs and kisses from my kids and grandkids. But I do shed a few tears when I put my hammock away and say goodbye to the margarita gals. La Perlita owns a big part of my heart."

"My last guests check out the first of May," Lisa says and adjusts the side view mirrors of the Chevy Blazer. "I'll head back north shortly thereafter."

Neither my niece nor I have ever contemplated living in La Perlita year-round, although some of our northern friends have started to do so. "I don't know how your mom tolerated summers here for so long—too hot for me," I say. "But even if I installed air conditioning to bear the heat, I wouldn't want to be away from my family. Five months a year is plenty."

Lisa straightens her blouse collar and then rolls down her window, obviously settling in for the forty-minute drive. "What's going to happen with the boat safety group you were putting together with Captain Ricardo?" she asks as we leave La Perlita in the rearview mirror.

I explain how Ricardo has met several times with the fishing associations and individual fishermen to tighten up safety regulations. He did not see the need for an outside committee, but put the idea of teaching ocean safety in the schools on his list of things to do.

"I hope he follows through with that," she says. "By the way, any more romantic sparks between you two?"

"Nope. It's better that way. Did I mention his dogs...?"

We share a belly laugh, which leaves me smiling as I gaze out the window enjoying the ocean views.

"Can you leave Alejandro's disappearance at rest now?"

"I have no choice but to stop my search. There's no answer. I hope for Rosy's sake he's alive somewhere. I believe the real answer lies with Captain Martin—but he and the other three recite the same story. Which means it's the truth or they made a pact to stick with a lie."

"If it's a lie...maybe, someday, one of them will break."

"Could be. Sergio promises to keep on top of it. Right now they refuse to discuss the matter with anybody. They won't even talk to Rosy or Cesar, who most deserve a conversation with them about that day."

A half hour later, I silently say goodbye to the blue Pacific, abundant bougainvillea, and swaying palms as we pass the city of Puerto Vallarta and head east. The serenity of beautiful beaches is now replaced by restaurants, hotels, commercial malls, and gated communities.

"Although some people in La Perlita still hold on to the cartel hit theory, I pray that didn't happen," I say. "The idea of Alejandro being murdered is just too much for my heart." I feel tears wanting to fall and take in a deep breath.

"There you go again. Sucking the oxygen out of the car," Lisa says.

I fill my lungs. Hold my breath for a long moment. And exhale one last noisy breath. And grin.

Laughing, Lisa pulls in front of the departure doors at the airport and turns off the engine. "One more question."

"Yes?" I say, my hand on the door handle.

"Don't you wonder why your buddy, the police chief, can tell you so assuredly that the cartel wasn't involved in Alejandro's disappearance?"

I pause to consider her question. "I've heard rumors. I'm not blind to the widespread corruption in Mexico— but I'm choosing to believe there are informants inside the cartel that let him know things."

"You are a very trusting soul, Auntie."

Lisa joins me curbside and helps offload my two fifty-pound suitcases. "What's in these?" she asks. "They're heavy."

I list out the sundry of items I'm carting north, including gifts for the kids and all my summer clothes, and end with, "and four big, decorative tequila bottles—full."

She shakes her head in disbelief. "The tequila isn't for you. That I know."

"You're right. They're a gift."

We hug one last time. "Safe travels," she says and gets back into her car.

I wave, take a deep breath, and drag my luggage into the airport.

My heart turns heavy.

Alejandro, where are you?

PART II

❧ TWENTY ❧

*W*here am I?

Alejandro awoke on a lumpy mattress under a coarse blanket, unsure how he got there. A moment of relief was followed by confusion. He opened his eyes enough to see a thatched roof that blocked the sun but not the sweltering, wet heat. He looked from right to left. Even that small movement caused him dizziness. Pushing the scratchy blanket to the side, he found himself naked, so he pulled the cover back over his groin area. Closing his eyes, he took a deep breath and thanked God for being off the rocking boat and on land, somewhere.

When he came to again, an elderly woman sat on the floor next to his mattress. Her gray hair fell over her shoulder in a long braid. Lines etched her weathered brown face. She cooed something to him in a soft, gentle voice, but he couldn't understand her language.

"Where am I?" he asked.

Friendly eyes and a toothless smile spoke of safety as her hands caressed his arm. The old woman babbled for a few minutes. Answering his question? She put a half-coconut shell to his lips. The sweet, cool water was a gift to his parched throat, although his sunbaked lips ached with the touch of the rough surface.

He longed to communicate with this woman, with anybody, but no matter how many times he asked about his whereabouts, all he got in return was babble.

He looked up at the thatched roof, guessing his whereabouts. Thatched roof. Humid. A lumpy, possibly straw, mattress. A burlap-type blanket. A dark-skinned, weathered woman. I must be in the tropics. Somewhere. Not Latin America, or she would have understood my questions. Where am I?

The next time Alejandro awoke he found himself in semi-darkness. The smell of onions and fish broth drew him into consciousness. He wiped saliva gathered on the side of his mouth and clutched the locket resting against his chest. The same woman sat at his side. With a swollen tongue, he touched his lips, feeling a slippery salve. He looked at her through strands of his long hair. "*¿Dónde estoy?*"

A gnarled, gentle hand touched his face. Dark brown eyes searched his. "Mona," she said, touching her chest. "Mona."

"Mona," Alejandro repeated and lay still. Mona must be her name.

The woman lifted more water to his mouth. He drank, thankful for the liquid. "Mona, where am I? Please. Do you understand anything I say?"

She spoke again as if to answer, but her words still confused him. He watched her reach towards him, a straight razor in her hands.

"No!" he stammered. Terror filled him and he attempted to sit up. Exhausted, he fell back.

The old woman came near his face again with the razor and lather. Her eyes were kind, and brightened when she smiled. She waited as if asking for his permission.

He nodded.

With care, she began scraping the long, thick, matted beard off his face.

Her kindness comforted him. At the gentle human touch, tears moistened his cheeks.

The waves crashed into the panga, rocking the vessel violently side to side, jolting him awake. Torrential rain soaked him. He clung onto the bench, feeling his fingers cramp. If he let go he'd be thrown overboard. Sharks circled in the water below. He screamed.

Awaking from the clutches of the nightmare, Alejandro clenched the rough blanket with both hands. Sweat beaded on his forehead and then ran into his eyes. The same old lady was at his side. He couldn't stop himself from shivering in the early morning hours, even though the woman mopped the sweat from his face and laid several more burlap blankets over him.

He moaned, feeling her fingers move through his now short hair in a motherly caress, and fell into a fitful sleep.

✿ TWENTY-ONE ✿

"The soup is ready, Bubu," Alma whispered to her grandmother, Mona, motioning to the pot on the crude brick stove.

Mona nodded and saw the boy stir. "Put some aside to cool, please," she said.

She and her two adult granddaughters, Alma and Betra, had taken turns watching over this lad through three days and two nights, ever since his small canoe-like boat had washed ashore a few meters from their house.

A few minutes later, the young man opened his eyes. She smiled at him and lifted his head. With care not to spill, she moved the small clay bowl toward his lips. He sipped the warm broth and whimpered. She imagined this was his first cooked food in a long, long time.

Sitting up and steadying himself, Alejandro reached for the bowl, but the woman held it from him. She spoke words he could not understand.

"*Más*" he begged.

She brought the soup to his lips again.

Desperate, he put his hands around the container and gulped down the broth. "*Más.*"

The woman, who he remembered called herself Mona, smiled at him but didn't move to refill the container. Instead, she laid her hands gently on his chest and pushed him back down, placing a small pillow behind his head.

Alejandro surveyed the humble, one-room house. It seemed to span six by six meters square. Dirt floor. Wooden beams supported wood-plank walls. The thatched roof was made of interwoven palm leaves. A piece of cloth hung in what must be the front door. Three other thin mattresses like the one he lay on were stacked against the far wall.

"More," he said, looking toward the pot simmering on a rustic brick stove top. He could smell the wood and coconut husks used for cooking. He hadn't eaten in days, too weak to catch food.

Alejandro was pleased the woman seemed to understand. She came forward with more food. This time the broth held small pieces of fish.

"*Gracias,*" Alejandro said, ready to devour the soup.

The woman, again, kept the bowl from him. She rubbed her stomach, made vomiting motions and gestured, "slowly."

He nodded that he understood and allowed her to hold the bowl while he took small sips until it was empty. With a full stomach, he fell back to sleep.

Sometime later, Alejandro felt the need to pee and opened his eyes. "Please. Where am I?" he asked.

"*Ljab mejele,*" the old woman said with a welcoming smile.

"I don't understand you. Do you speak Spanish? Maybe some English?"

"*Ljab mejele.*"

"*No entiendo.*" He wanted to scream in frustration. Embarrassed, but not wanting to urinate under the blanket, he motioned toward an empty bottle lying nearby. Thankfully, the woman understood, brought it to him, and left the room.

After relieving himself, he placed the bottle near the side of the mattress and settled back under the blanket. He noticed the pot still on the stove near the home's entrance. He smelled onions, chili, and savory vegetables. His stomach rumbled.

Moments later, the woman returned. "*Etam?*" she asked, pointing to Alejandro. He looked at her without responding. She pointed to herself. "Mona." Then she touched his chest. "*Etam?*"

Alejandro understood she was asking his name. "Alejandro," he replied. "Alejandro Garcia."

Mona smiled. "Alejandro." She grasped his hands in hers. "*Iọkwe.*"

That must be a greeting, he thought. "*Iọkwe,*" he said in response, knowing he'd probably mispronounced it.

"*Iọkwe,*" Mona repeated, delight written on her face.

A young woman approached, sat on a floor mat by his mattress, and handed Alejandro liquid in a half coconut shell. "*Ni,*" she said.

He tasted it. Sweet, cool coconut juice. "*Ni. Gracias.*"

"Betra," the young woman said, pointing to herself. "Betra."

Alejandro responded with his own name.

Short, with mahogany-colored skin, expressive dark eyes, and long black hair, Betra seemed about his age. He saw her looking at his locket with kind eyes. He felt her inquisitiveness—as if asking permission to touch it. He nodded and Betra lifted the pendant off his chest, looked at him one more time, and opened it.

"Nando," Alejandro said, and used the back of his hand to wipe tears that began to fall. "*Mi* Nando. *Mi hijo.*" He touched a hand to his chest and then signaled, "smaller."

He then closed the locket and placed it back near his heart.

Alejandro watched Betra stand and walk to the corner of the room. She returned with a pair of shorts. He touched the cotton material and smiled. "*Gracias.*"

"*Jouj,*" Betra said. She retrieved the urine bottle before she and Mona walked out of the house.

"*Juyged?* You're welcome?" he wondered aloud. He did understand Betra wanted him to put on the shorts. Removing the coarse blanket, he pulled them up his legs to his waist, grateful to cover his nakedness. His arms looked like bamboo stalks, dark and thin. His thighs were reduced to the size of his forearms.

"These shorts would fit a ten-year-old," he muttered, and tied the drawstring. "And still they're big on me."

Alejandro attempted to stand but fell forward onto his knees. He knocked over a clay pot of fresh flowers set on a metal stand next to his bed.

The noise brought Betra, Mona and another woman running back into the house. Together they took him by his arms and laid him back onto the mattress.

Moving onto his side, Alejandro curled into the fetal position. Overcome by exhaustion and emotion, he let the tears fall. "*¿Dónde estoy?*"

Mona smiled and with tender care began to apply what smelled like coconut oil on his back, legs, and swollen feet.

Hoping the women knew some English, he asked, "Where am I?"

In response came chatter that sounded like a native Indian language he had heard long ago in television movies.

❧ TWENTY-TWO ❧

Often, Mona pondered the mystery of the young castaway. A week after her granddaughters had found him emaciated and unconscious in a shallow canoe, he had regained enough strength to sit and stand without assistance.

She taught him Alma's name and used hand signs to explain that she was their *bubu*, grandmother.

Trained by her mother in healing practices, Mona mashed papaya skin to treat his severe burns and mixed a potion of papaya, flowers, and coconut oil for his chapped, swollen face. She directed her granddaughters to apply coconut oil to his skin and massage his calloused hands and bruised feet.

Throughout the day Mona plied him with liquids to reduce his dehydration and at night, she served him mint and lemongrass tea to help him sleep in comfort.

"Even with our care and ointments, he still cries out at night and thrashes about in pain, Bubu," Betra whispered late one night. "What else can we do besides sit with him?"

"We must wait. His healing will take a long time."

"Shouldn't we tell the town leaders?" Alma asked. She was brushing her long brown hair, preparing to braid it.

"No. Tell no one about the young man," Mona cautioned. "Especially when you go into town for supplies, Alma."

"Why, Bubu?" Alma asked. "He's a miracle. Shouldn't people know?"

"Even though Namu is very small, word will spread around the village and among the fishermen to other islands," her grandmother said. "Many people will storm our land and our home to gawk, poke and question. That will not be good. It is too soon."

Alma finished her hair and lay down to sleep. "Yes, Bubu. It is best we keep him a secret."

"I agree," Betra said. "Years ago, a man was found on Ebon. Remember? There was much commotion. The authorities and press from around the world surrounded him. Some believed him. Others accused him of a lie. The family of the second man on that boat, who died, accused the survivor of eating him or something! It was not good. We must protect Alejandro. It is too soon for him to have so much attention."

On a hot muggy morning in late March, two weeks after Alejandro's abrupt entrance into their lives, Mona and Betra sat with Alejandro on the sand outside the house. Mona watched him stare blankly out into the ocean.

Her mother's heart longed to comfort him, but she didn't know how. She felt his longing to know where he was, but the language barrier was too wide.

"Betra, give this to Alma," she said, handing her youngest granddaughter a tan-colored mat she had just finished weaving. "Tell her to put it into the bag with the others to take to town this morning."

"Yes, Bubu," Betra responded and disappeared into the house.

Fifteen years ago, the beach where they sat had been three times as wide. But year after year, the ocean had drawn nearer. Now, at high tide, the waves crashed upon the brick barricade they had erected outside their home, and at times seawater washed in through the front entrance. Mona wondered how much longer before her island would be under water.

A few meters to her left, partially pulled onto shore, sat the young man's boat. Its hull was encrusted with barnacles, algae, and mussels. They had found some turtle shells and fish bones inside. Scraps of material fluttered off a pole on the bow like a ripped sail.

Given his appearance, she knew he'd been in that boat for a long, long time. Betra had found 270 short, straight lines carved on the bench. "Was he drifting all those days?" Mona wondered. "Where did he come from?"

Picking up a stick, she drew a circle in the damp sand. "Here," she said, pointing. "Here. Namu."

Alejandro looked at her, questions in his tired eyes.

She pointed to the circle again. "Namu."

"Namu," he repeated. "*Aquí.* Namu."

She nodded her head and smiled her big toothless grin.

Coming back out of the house, Betra tucked loose strands of hair behind her ears and sat on the other side of Alejandro. Years earlier, she and Alma had attended school in the small village, a thirty-minute walk from their home. Before leaving the sixth grade to help her grandmother care for her ailing grandfather, Betra had learned to read a map. She knew where Namu and the other Marshall Islands were situated in relation to neighboring countries in the North and South Pacific.

Asking her *bubu* for the stick, she drew the big land mass of Australia, far away to the left of Namu, and then small circles near and around their island. She, her widowed grandmother, and sister lived on one of the isolated outer coral reefs over three hundred miles away by boat from the urban center of Majuro. Her parents had died in a ferry accident on the way to Majuro when she and Alma were still in grammar school.

She didn't know how to explain Namu to Alejandro. And she didn't know which island or country he had come from.

Betra noticed Alejandro stare at the sand, watching her draw circle after circle with the stick. The more she drew, the more his eyes lit up. She hoped he was starting to realize he was on an island among many others.

She began naming the coral reefs that made up the Marshall Islands as she had learned them in school: "Ailik, Arno, Aur, Ebon, Enewetak, Namorik, Namu..." stopping short of naming and drawing all of the twenty-four inhabited municipalities and the 1,200 outer islands.

"Mexico?" he asked.

"Mayheco?" Betra repeated with a questioning look.

Alejandro took the stick from her hands and wrote M E X I C O in the sand.

Betra smiled when Alejandro handed the stick back to her. She cleared the sand with her hand and drew a tiny circle for Namu in the middle, a big one for Australia a foot to the left, and then got up and walked toward the water. "Ocean," she said, pointing at the water. She used her fingers and made wavy lines in the sand to represent the sea.

Alejandro nodded as if he understood, and said, "*El océano*."

Then a foot to the right of Namu, across empty sand, she drew a line to represent a coast and wrote USA first and under that she wrote, M E X I C O.

Alejandro nodded his understanding, placed his face in his hands, and slumped his shoulders.

"A long way away," Betra said, knowing he couldn't understand her.

Mona touched Betra on the shoulder and gestured toward Alejandro. "Enough now. The lad is tired."

"Yes, Bubu." Betra offered Alejandro her hand for support in standing. She then used both hands to represent "sleep" and guided him into the house to his mattress.

Later that evening, while Alma cleaned up the dinner dishes, Alejandro took a short walk with Betra. He had so many questions for this family of three who had saved his life, but no way to ask them. He wondered why there was no man around, where the nearest neighbor would be, and why nobody ever came to visit. He wanted to know where the girls' parents were and how the three women made a living. Most importantly, he wanted to ask how he could contact his family.

He had seen Alma leave in the mornings with a bulging cloth bag hanging from her shoulder. She returned before dinner with her bag full of food. He wondered where she went.

Slender, with long brown hair kept in a braid, Alma stood six inches taller than Betra. Where Betra's eyes sparkled with delight at the slightest thing, Alma seemed serious and sad. "Definitely the older sister," Alejandro mused.

His strength returned little by little, which encouraged him. But he couldn't fathom how he would ever communicate with his hosts or find his way home.

On their walk, Alejandro and Betra passed the *panga* where he had survived for over nine months—270 marks—although he knew at one point he had stopped counting, too weak to stay awake, almost too weak to breathe. He stopped and looked at the *panga*. Painful memories overwhelmed him.

He remembered the first day he caught a white albatross that had landed on the boat's bow. Desperately hungry, he had prepared carefully for the catch. He cut off a portion of the material he'd used for shade and tied the corners together. He readied it like a large bonnet. It took him many tries over several days but when the fifth albatross perched, he lurched and cast—scooping the seabird inside the material.

Alejandro smiled for a second, remembering his shout of victory that day.

There weren't many good moments to remember.

Strolling down the beach, he marveled at the isolation of the island. Palm trees lined the water's edge, birds chirped within the fronds, and the clear turquoise water lapped over pink and white coral. There was not a soul or a house around for as far as his eyes could see. How deserted was this island?

Betra walked into the water to refresh her face and retrieved a floating coconut shell. She motioned for him to follow her.

The thought of entering the ocean petrified him. He shook his head. No. He couldn't.

Betra seemed to understand. Returning to his side,

she took his hand and walked further inland, five minutes away—to a small orchard filled with banana, papaya, and coconut trees.

"*Ni,*" she said, showing him the coconut.

"*Coco,*" he responded. Smiling he picked a banana from a tree and pronounced, "bah nah na."

"*Pinana,*" she replied and laughed.

This was followed by the words in Marshallese and Spanish for papaya, the sand, the sea, and the sky.

They picked fruit, which Betra gathered in the bottom half of her long skirt—using it as a basket—and headed back to the house. Approaching the *panga* again, Alejandro stopped. He took a deep breath and pulled the vessel further onto the shore. The effort exhausted him. Bent over with his hands on his knees, he calmed his breathing, rested for a moment, and then stepped in. He yanked on and retrieved a small package tied to a cleat.

Stepping back onto the sand, he noticed Betra's curious expression.

Alejandro untied the ragged piece of cloth to show Betra his cell phone, with its rusted metal edges. Using words and pantomime he questioned, "Is there anywhere to make a phone call?"

Betra looked at Alejandro and the phone. "No," she said with a sad face. "No."

He used his fingers to mimic typing and watched Betra for an expression.

She shook her head. "No."

That night, Alejandro tossed and turned, unable to sleep. He now knew he was a long way from home, across that huge ocean. The thought of being in a boat again terrified him. How could he ever get home? He wanted to call his mother and brother or send them a text. He wanted to talk to Nando. But there was no phone, no internet, and no seeming connection with the outside world.

It had been so long since he'd spoken on the phone, sent a text, or even communicated with somebody in his own language. "Well, I did talk to the *panga* and Charlie the turtle," he reminded himself. That thought made him want to both laugh and cry.

He thought back to his life in La Perlita. To his obsession with texting and selfies. To his partying, drinking almost every night after Maria left him, and all the women he used to cover the hurt and emptiness he felt inside.

Am I still that person? If not, who am I?

Alejandro cradled the locket in his hand, opened it to kiss Nando's picture, and then held it close to his heart as he had done every night for over 270 nights. He recited the Lord's Prayer, "*Padre nuestro, que está en el cielo...*" and thanked God for keeping him alive. He prayed for a way to return home.

❧ TWENTY-THREE ❧

Days passed. Alejandro had no way of knowing the exact date, but calculated he had been in Namu with Mona and her daughters for nearly a month. He felt stronger each day under Mona's care and looked forward to each meal. Some of the ingredients Mona used were unfamiliar, like the leaves from the pandanus tree Betra had shown him in their small orchard. The leaves that Mona and Alma used to wrap sticky rice and fish in had an herbal, floral-like aroma. They also made fire-roasted breadfruit— wrapping it in banana leaves and cooking it over the open fire. He particularly liked mashed *taro,* which reminded him of potatoes and home.

The shorts he had been wearing no longer fit, so Alma brought him bigger ones. From somewhere they gifted him a pair of leather sandals and a t-shirt that said, "Olympic Games 2008."

Daily he walked with Betra into the orchard to pick fruit. Each time, he stopped by the *panga* for a moment to reflect and thank God he had survived the ordeal. Having had no experience as a seaman, he knew his survival was a miracle.

How would he ever explain the pain, the desperation, the hunger, the terror? He had forced himself to eat raw seabirds, turtles, and fish. With bare hands or the "net" he'd roughly fashioned, he had grabbed any living thing that came near the boat. He cut into it with his knife to remove the innards and then gulped down the raw meat. When the sun was out, he dried the fish and seabird entrails—liver, brain, heart—for separate meals. He severed fish heads and ate them with the eyes intact. He drank the turtle blood and used the empty turtle shell to collect rainwater.

How could he explain this fight for survival? Who would believe that he talked to the *panga* and to the empty turtle shell to keep his sanity? Or the panic he felt when waves crashed into the boat, threatening to wash him overboard to be eaten by the sharks that circled—lurking, waiting.

One hot, muggy afternoon, Alejandro rested in the shade next to the house fanning his face with a palm leaf while Mona continued her weaving. Betra stepped out of the cool ocean water, smiled, flicked water at him, and sat down.

She continued her daily lessons, teaching him words in her language. He now understood that *Iqkwe* meant both *hola* and *adios*. Something that sounded like "hey man ur?" meant *¿cómo está? Aet* meant *sí,* and *jab* meant *no.*

Betra asked him many questions in pantomime he didn't understand. Others he guessed at and answered by drawing in the wet sand, like her question about his family.

"*Mi familia,*" he had said, drawing stick figures of his mother, stepfather, brother and sister.

In turn, she drew a man, woman, and small child, grouped them in a circle and pointed at him with questioning eyes.

"*Jab.* No," he said in response. Taking the stick from Betra's hands he crossed out the woman and drew her with another man. He didn't know if she understood him or not.

Betra went on to draw a man, woman, and two little girls. He understood these were her parents, her sister, and herself. She crossed out the man and woman and pointed to the sky with sadness in her eyes.

"I'm sorry," he said, now understanding her parents were dead. There was no way to ask her what happened.

Wondering about her grandfather, Alejandro drew two stick figures and wrote M O N A above one of the two.

Betra crossed out the man next to Mona and indicated he also was in heaven.

"*Lo siento,*" he said, placing his hand over his heart.

Earlier that day, Alejandro had watched Alma again disappear down the dusty road in the opposite direction from the orchard. "Where. Alma. Go?" he had asked Betra in their pantomime way of communicating.

She drew a long line in the sand and then a big circle with houses.

"*Pueblo grande?*" he asked and drew a bigger circle with lots of buildings in the middle.

She shook her head and used her hands to mime that it was neither too small nor too big.

Excited, Alejandro brought out the cell phone sitting in his pocket. "Call? *Mi familia?*"

Betra raised both hands palms up and shrugged her shoulders. "*Bolen.*"

He assumed she was saying, "Maybe," and stood up, ready to walk down the road and find out.

Betra stopped him with a shake of her head, "*Jab*. No." She then gestured it was a very long walk and Alejandro was too weak.

Alejandro clenched his fists and jaw. A town existed. He might be able to communicate with his family. He wanted to go. Could he make the walk?

Betra took his arm and held him tight.

He tried to break away but was too weak to fight her. He sat back down and put his head between his knees and punched the sand. He felt Betra's caresses on his upper back as he took in deep breaths to calm down.

Betra lifted his chin gently, looked into his eyes, and said words that he somehow understood, "*Jab*. Not yet. Soon."

"*Pronto*," he promised himself.

That evening, Alejandro was using seashells to teach Betra to count in Spanish when he saw two people approach on a small motorcycle. He recognized Alma on the back of the bike and jumped to his feet. His fast movement made him dizzy. Betra steadied him.

"*Iqkwe*," the man said, engaging the kickstand.

Within moments of dismounting, Alma was at his side with a big smile. Mona walked out of the house, straightening her long skirt.

A flurry of words flowed around Alejandro. He heard the words "*Etam*" and "Alejandro," and knew the man had asked his name and Mona had provided it.

He watched facial expressions and body language for clues to the conversation. The smiles assured Alejandro this was a friendly visit. He watched Betra point to the *panga* and back at him.

"*Mi nombre Jarom,*" the man said.

"*¿Hablas español?*" Alejandro said, shocked but thrilled to hear his language spoken.

"*Sí. Poco.* And some English."

"I come from Majuro, the capital city," Jarom said. "Alma asked somebody in the village center yesterday to radio over, asking for my immediate assistance." He looked with fondness at Mona. "I cared for Mona's husband many years ago and feared she was now sick. I left early this morning to get here."

Alma's actions touched Alejandro's heart. He smiled at her and said, "*Kumolo,*" which he had learned meant, "*Gracias.*"

She smiled back and nodded. "*Jiu.*"

Alejandro invited Jarom to sit with him on a bench in the shade. Using English, Spanish, and some drawing in the sand, Alejandro attempted to explain his terrifying journey. How he had been fishing with a small crew off the coast of Nayarit, Mexico, in June when the motor failed. He told Jarom his captain had instructed him to stay behind in the *panga* while he and others gathered the fish off the long-line. Before they returned, a strong wind and rolling waves had pulled the *panga* away from the anchoring buoy. The material he had hung for shade caught the wind, moving him further away.

Overwhelmed by the memory, Alejandro stopped talking. He clasped his hands together to stop them from shaking.

Betra sat down next to Alejandro. Her presence comforted him, and he reached for her hand.

"You have suffered a terrible ordeal," Jarom said. "I am a doctor. May I examine you?"

Mona took the doctor's and Alejandro's hands in hers and led them into the house. She left them alone.

Dr. Jarom opened the backpack slung over his shoulder. Taking out some instruments, he checked Alejandro's temperature and blood pressure. "*Muy bien*," he said. He took a stethoscope out of the backpack and said, "*Tos, por favor.*"

Alejandro coughed as requested.

"*Excelente.*" Jarom put his instruments away. "Two hundred and seventy days?" he asked, raising his eyebrows.

"*Sí.* Maybe more."

The doctor checked Alejandro's skin, top to bottom, and then looked into his mouth. He checked his teeth and looked for any white spots that would indicate ulcers. "Everything looks good. What a miracle this is."

"*Sí, un milagro,*" Alejandro responded, making the sign of the cross. "Mona and Betra and Alma. Good care," he said and smiled.

"You look healthy—although your feet are still somewhat swollen. Your wounds are healing. You have a couple of loose teeth from malnutrition. I'd like to do some blood work at my clinic. And I'm sure the foreign affairs officer will want to talk to you. And newspaper reporters," Dr. Jarom said. "I'm only the first of many who will want to meet you."

Alejandro shook his head, confusion written on his face. "Clinic? Reporters? *¿Dónde?*"

"Majuro. There's a ferry out late this evening and one tomorrow. There won't be another one until next week. You can't walk to the boat dock in the village yet, but I could take you on the rented motorcycle. It's then eight hours on a ferry across the ocean to Majuro."

"*¿Agua? ¿Ocho horas? No.*" The color drained from Alejandro's face and his hands began to shake. He crumbled onto the mattress and cried out, "No! I can't!"

Betra heard Alejandro's anguished scream and rushed into the house. She knelt next to him and put protective arms around him. "What happened?" she asked, looking up at the doctor.

"I told him I'd like to finish my exam in Majuro, which means getting him there by ferry, and he collapsed. Even if we get money from government officials to fly him to Majuro, he still has to island hop, at least to the airstrip in Ebon."

Betra nodded while still holding Alejandro tight, wanting to shield him from any harm.

"He must go over water. I'm sorry. There's no other way out of here," Jarom said.

Betra shook her head. "We'll keep him here a while longer. Alma contacted you so you could examine him, not take him away. Thank you for coming. I know it's a miracle he survived so long at sea, but please do not invade our privacy by bringing other people here. He's not ready."

"This is a miracle story, Betra," the doctor said. "The world will want to know. Doctors will want to document his survival. This all needs to be investigated for its truthfulness. His family needs to be notified. Aren't you being selfish keeping him here?"

"We understand all that. My grandmother, sister and I have discussed this at length from the first day. Alejandro is traumatized. He cries out at night. He is regaining strength and sleeping a few hours a night, but it is too soon to turn him over to the outside world."

Dr. Jarom accepted Mona's invitation to dinner—grilled tuna—which Alma had received in trade for two of their hand-woven mats. Mona prepared steaming white rice and taro to compliment the fresh fish.

Taking advantage of the doctor's language skills, Alejandro asked about the death of Betra's parents.

"They were on the way to Majuro to visit my son-in-law's parents. An unexpected hurricane hit." Mona breathed in deeply. "The ferry sunk. Eighty-five people drowned."

Grief shrouded her face and crept into her eyes. After Jarom translated the answer, Alejandro was sorry he had asked the question.

"It was a long time ago. It feels like yesterday," Alma said.

"Tell me about the town Alma walks to almost every day," Alejandro asked to change the subject.

"It is small," Dr. Jarom said. "Maybe two thousand inhabitants."

"That is tiny," Alejandro said. "La Perlita is small and we have five thousand people."

"But we have everything we need," Alma interjected. "A fresh fish market, an elementary school, and an arts and crafts market. Visitors come from Ebon to buy handmade mats, hammocks, leather sandals and embroidered clothing."

Surprised, Alejandro said, "There are visitors on this island? Nobody has ever come near here."

"That's because there is a strict rule on the outer atolls," Jarom explained. "To visit other islands, you need permission from a local family to be on their land, but it's not easy getting that permission."

He looked at Mona and smiled. "Right, Mona?"

She nodded. "We are a simple people. We do not want influence from the outside world. This has been our way for generations."

"For their economic survival, the villagers voted to allow outsiders to come shop, but they must not go outside the market area. It's hard to imagine for some, Alejandro, but life on these outer islands is primitive. But, like Mona says, they want it this way. No television, phones, internet, or tourist facilities."

"This is what we know. How we live," Betra explained to Alejandro. "We like it—most of the time. But sometimes, I want to know more. See more. Experience more."

"We are fine. Just the way we are. This is God's will for our lives," Jarom translated as Mona spoke to Betra and Alma.

Alejandro wondered if that was indeed true. He was just getting to know Betra, but she seemed much too alive, too restless, to be content to spend all her days here on this remote island.

Preparing to leave a while later, Jarom shook Alejandro's hand. "I'll be back in a couple of weeks," he said.

"Thank you. Please take this," Alejandro said, handing the doctor his cell phone. "My family is in La Perlita, Jalisco, Mexico. I don't know their phone numbers by memory. But they're in the phone. My mother, Rosy, is listed under 'Mamá.' My brother, Cesar, is listed as 'Carnal,' which means hermano."

Alejandro took a deep breath. "Tell them I am alive and will be home soon. *Por favor.*"

Dr. Jarom examined the phone. "It looks damaged. What if I can't access the numbers?"

"Please call our village mayor. *El delegado.* His name is Jose Zamora. He knows my family. He will give them the message."

Mona took the doctor's hands in hers. "Thank you for coming to examine Alejandro. Please keep his presence here confidential for now. This is my home. I will not allow anybody to come onto my land. Do you understand?"

"Yes, ma'am," the doctor said.

That night Mona gave Alejandro herb tea to help him sleep. After hearing his snores, she and her daughters sat outside under the stars. The full moon illuminated their faces.

"Was it a mistake to ask the doctor to come?" Alma asked her grandmother.

"No. It is good we made a first contact. We can't hide him forever. I pray others won't come looking for him, though." Mona pulled the hem of her skirt down to her ankles, away from mosquitoes and sand fleas. "His physical body is almost ready to leave," she said. "But he has ocean demons in his mind."

"How can he get ready to cross the sea? At least to Ebon?" Alma asked.

Betra ran her fingers through the sand. Tears ran down her cheeks and onto the ground.

"Why do you cry, little sister?"

"Because...I...I don't want him to leave," Betra whispered. "I've fallen in love with him."

Alma touched Betra's hand and gave it a gentle squeeze. "I know you have, and I'd wager he has similar feelings for you."

"It may be love. It may be compassion," Mona said with a kind smile. "You have such a good heart. You always have. Even your name means 'love.'"

She looked at both of her granddaughters and took their hands in hers. "You both have caring spirits. But he can't stay here. He has a family. A son."

"But not a wife."

"How do you know that, Betra?" Alma asked with surprise in her voice.

"We've talked about it. He drew me a picture in the sand—of his mother, brother, sister, and his son, Nando." Betra took a deep breath. "When I drew a picture of him, a wife and his son, he crossed out the wife and drew her separately with somebody else...another man."

Alma laughed. "Who says we need a common language to communicate? You two seem to have done just fine while I'm off in the village square selling our fruit, coconuts, and mats."

Betra looked at her sister, guilt written on her face. "I'm sorry I left you to do that by yourself this last month. Alejandro needed me."

Alma reached over and hugged her sister. "Yes, he did, and you and Bubu have worked miracles with him."

Mona took Betra's hands in her own. "Now we need to heal his mind, remove the terrifying memories, and help him lose his fear of the ocean."

"I'll let you work on his mind, Bubu," Betra said, looking at her grandmother with affection. "But I have an idea to help him lose some of his fear of the sea. We'll start tomorrow."

~ TWENTY-FOUR ~

Alejandro awoke in the middle of the night and couldn't get back to sleep. He tossed and turned, wishing Mona's tea had worked its magic for the entire night.

"By tomorrow my family will know I'm alive," he reminded himself. Excitement flowed like an electrical current through him, as he envisioned his family screaming and crying with joy.

He imagined Nando's face and longed to hold and kiss him.

Will he remember me? That thought turned his excitement into sadness. What if he doesn't know me? What if he sees his mommy's new boyfriend as his daddy now? His sadness turned to devastation. With worry on his mind, he fell back to sleep.

He dreamed he was on the *panga*, vomiting over the side as the boat rocked to and fro.

Crowing roosters startled Betra, and she jumped out of bed. She was usually up before dawn to help her mother and sister feed the pigs and chickens and gather eggs. But not this morning. She had laid awake most of the night listening to Alejandro toss, turn, and moan. At one point she heard him gag like he might vomit, and she ran to his mattress. She laid down beside him and held his hand in comfort until he went into a deep sleep.

"Good morning, Bubu," Betra said, giving her grand-mother a hug outside their front door.

"Good morning. You slept later than usual."

"I stayed awake, concerned about Alejandro. He had a hard night."

"I heard him as well. Tonight I will brew him a stron-ger tea. I'm sure thoughts of his family kept him awake." Mona paused and wiped her hands on her apron. "I saw you go to his bed. Is that wise?"

"He suffers. I want to comfort him."

"I understand that. But be careful. We really know nothing about him."

"He is a good man. I can feel it."

"He is a man, with man's desires. And you are a naïve young girl."

"Please, Bubu," Betra begged. "I trust him. He will not harm me."

"I won't forbid you, but I will watch out for you. Now go bring me some eggs for breakfast. And gather some herbs from the garden."

Betra did as she was asked, stopping to greet her sis-ter who was washing her hands and face in a bucket by the well.

"I watched you go to Alejandro last night," Alma said. "Grandmother is right. He has many demons."

"Yes, he does. I can't even imagine the horrors of being alone on a small boat for so long. Baking in the sun. Hungry. Terrified. Those nightmares are going to be inside him for a long time."

"Do you think it wise to go to his bed, little sister? Even though you have twenty-two years, you are innocent.

Like a child. Remember, he won't be with us forever—he needs to return to his family."

"I've never had these feelings before, Alma. It feels good to care about somebody this deeply. I want to shelter him. Protect him. Is this how you felt about Michael?"

"Don't compare Alejandro to Michael," Alma said with a stern voice. "Michael was one of us. From Ebon. From our culture. When he left to work in the United States and didn't return...well, you know that broke my heart. You can't trust men to stay. It is best to keep your distance. I don't want you sad and alone, too. Someday you'll meet somebody who is right for you."

Betra wiped a tear from her cheek. "I don't think so. We are so isolated here on Namu. Young boys leave when they become men. You wouldn't have met Michael if he hadn't come to Namu to visit his uncle during our town festival."

Betra saw her sister's eyes fill with sadness, but she continued, "Then, after he asked you to marry him and promised you the moon, he left. There is no future here."

Alma put her hands on Betra's shoulders and looked into her eyes. "Are you making Alejandro fall in love with you so that he'll take you away...to his country?"

"No! That is not my intention. But if it happens, I will go."

Alma shook her head in disbelief. "And leave your grandmother?"

Betra picked up the egg basket and squared her shoulders. "Do you want me to stay here alone forever?"

"You are not alone. We are a family. We promised grandfather on his deathbed to take care of Bubu. You can't just leave." Alma looked off into the distance. "At least Michael promised to come and live here with us after we married. Maybe he'll come back someday."

"Oh, my sister. Are you still holding on to that hope, after two years?"

Tears filled Alma's eyes. "Maybe."

Betra steeled herself. "Well, I can't live on hope alone. Anyway, Grandmother is waiting. We'll talk later."

As Betra started to walk away, Alma said, "Last night you said you have an idea on how to help Alejandro with his demons. What is your plan?"

"You'll see. After he wakes up and we have breakfast I'll show you. But right now, I need to collect eggs and herbs for Bubu."

Two hours later, Betra gestured for Alejandro to sit on the sand in front of the house. Mona and Alma stood in the doorway watching. Betra brought a bucket of seawater and set it at Alejandro's feet. "Water good," she said, with a bright smile.

Alejandro stared at her.

Sitting next to him she raised the bucket and slowly poured the water onto his feet. "Water good," she repeated.

Alejandro nodded as if he understood.

She stood and took Alejandro's hand inviting him to join her. Removing her sandals, she gestured for him to do the same. She then led him to the ocean's edge.

"Water good," she said a third time.

She guided him two steps forward, watching the gentle waves wash over their feet. She gave him a big smile.

He stood motionless.

Feeling the ocean waves lap gently, Betra sat in the shallow water and invited him to do the same. She placed her hand on his thigh to comfort him. Minutes later, when she felt some of the tension leave his body, she scooted forward. He followed until the water covered their legs.

She went no further. Releasing Alejandro's hand, she began to scoop the water in her hands and refresh her arms. And waited.

Moments later he also rinsed the ocean water over his arms.

She gave him a big smile. Enough for one day, she thought. This is good.

Alejandro stayed in the water next to Betra for several minutes, taking deep breaths and steeling himself. *I can do this. I have to do this. I must find a way back to my family.*

Determined, he stood and offered Betra his hand. She looked up at him with surprise and jumped to her feet at his invitation.

The joy on her face gave him resolve. He guided her deeper into the ocean until the water reached his knees. Her smile lit up her dark eyes and he felt love surge through him. Maybe I don't need to leave, he thought. I could just stay here and ask Betra to marry me. I would never need to cross the ocean. I can pull in the fish nets, work in the orchard, and help Alma sell fruits and vegetables in the village.

Hundreds of thoughts and feelings—from love to worry and fear—covered him like the water cascading down his face as Betra poured handfuls of water onto his head. Reaching out, he took hold of her hands, pulled her forward and held her in a tight embrace.

❧ TWENTY-FIVE ❧

"Betra. *Ven. Mi casa*," Alejandro whispered as they stood on the beach in the moonlight that night. He took her hands into his and caressed the palms. Betra's smile took his breath away. "You. Me. *Juntos*."

"*Juntos*," she repeated, touching first her heart and then his. "*Lippān doon.*"

She stepped closer and laid her head on his shoulder. She smelled of lavender and coconut. Light from the full moon shimmered on the water in front of them, reflecting blue-green hues gently lapping on the shore.

Overwhelmed with emotion he had never expected to feel again, Alejandro turned slightly to gaze into Betra's eyes. He found love and acceptance. He took her face in his hands and pulled her closer, capturing her lips in his. Their first kiss sent electrical bolts of raw energy through his body. He deepened the kiss, enjoying Betra's response—first delicate kisses, then more urgent ones coming alive with passion. He welcomed her in his arms as she pressed her body against his.

Her spontaneous groan of desire reached inside him. It touched and burst through the door to his heart he had closed a year earlier. The heart he had closed tight against pain and disappointment when Maria took Nando and left.

Embracing Betra, he guided her down onto the warm sand. Rolling onto his side to face her, he gazed into her welcoming eyes. He caressed her cheek, ran his fingers down her jawline, and his thumb over her bottom lip now swollen from the pressure of their kisses.

"How do I tell you all I am feeling?" he said. "You, Mona, and Alma saved my life. You protected me and nursed me back to health." Tears of gratitude sprang to his eyes.

Betra's look of confusion affirmed she did not understand all his words, but even so, she embraced him tightly.

Alejandro knew he felt more than gratitude. This beautiful, tropical, dark-skinned island girl with her big expressive eyes had softened hard places in his heart. Over the last two months, she had become his emotional lifeline. *How can I leave here without her?*

He kissed her again, deeper this time...moaning as she opened her mouth to receive him, caressing his tongue with hers.

Sensing her readiness to share these intimate pleasures, Alejandro raised the hem of Betra's skirt and moved his hand up her smooth, warm legs. His body tingled with erotic sensations.

Betra answered his advances, pressing her body closer to his.

"Betra? Alejandro?"

Alejandro moved away from Betra. His passion deflated like air from a pierced balloon.

"We are here, Bubu," Betra said, as she pulled the hem of her skirt back down to her ankles and ran fingers through her long hair. "Here. By the palm."

"It is late. Please come into the house."

"*Aet*, Bubu."

Alejandro stood and followed Betra down the beach and into the house to find Mona and Alma waiting with hot chocolate and sweet bread.

Hours later, Alejandro lay on his mattress in the small house now ensconced in darkness— except for a faint glow from the fire embers across the room. He could hear Mona snoring lightly from her mattress.

Sleep eluded him. "*Dulce y amargo*," he murmured. Sweet and sour, like that dish at the Chinese restaurant in La Perlita, he thought. As he contemplated his future, a sweetness warmed him. He thought about being back in La Perlita with his son, mother, and brother. But leave Betra behind? The thought soured his stomach. Can I take her with me? Would she go with me?

His musings were interrupted by Betra's presence. She knelt beside him, lifted the burlap blanket and without a sound slid into bed next to him. She laid her head on his chest and hugged him tightly.

Alejandro's stomach tightened and his pulse quickened. The stirrings he had felt back on the beach now throbbed within him.

"Betra." He whispered her name and then captured her lips in his. He began to explore her body.

"No," she said, grasping his hands in hers. "Sleep."

"Sleep? How? I want you." He kissed her neck and raised the hem of her nightdress, knowing they would be beginning a journey without return.

"Not yet. Time," she whispered in Spanish.

Her words stopped him. He smiled that she was disagreeing with him in his own language. How can I make her understand that time is running out? I will leave soon.

Frustrated, Alejandro lay awake as Betra fell asleep in his arms. He ached to make love to her. *She is not like other girls I have known. She is so innocent.* He took a deep breath. *I can't disrespect her or Mona.* Her presence comforted him, and he was soon asleep. When he awoke hours later, Betra was gone from his bed.

He began to make plans. Together with Betra at his side, he knew he could cross the ocean to Ebon, get onto an airplane, and return to La Perlita—not yet...but soon.

Each day he and Betra walked into the ocean, venturing further and further out. Together, holding hands. He no longer froze when the water reached his waist. Within days he stood in water up to his chest before the anxiety took his breath away, forcing him to return to shore.

"*Juntos,*" he told Betra, feeling it was only a matter of time before he would conquer his fear.

"*Juntos,*" she replied and held him close.

Days later, Alejandro dove into the waves and swam back to shore with Betra at his side. The couple hugged and laughed while Mona and Alma stood on the shore applauding.

The two worked, ate, and played together, *juntos,* during the day. They caught fish, picked fruit from the orchard, practiced each other's language, and helped Mona around the house. Alejandro used pieces of lumber Alma brought from town and repaired a rotting side wall. Using cement blocks and mortar he found behind the house, he replaced loose bricks at the front of the house and used palm fronds to fill in holes in the palapa ceiling.

And late each night, Betra would crawl into his bed and stay there in his arms until the wee morning hours before returning to her own mattress. Her presence worked better than Mona's herbal teas, and his night-mares vanished. He knew Mona and Alma must know she was in his bed, and he made sure to be respectful.

Alejandro finally worked up the confidence to ask Mona's permission to marry Betra and take her to Mexico. As much as he'd like to stay in Namu, he could not aban-don his son or his mother. But first, he needed Dr. Jarom to return with word from his family and money to get him home.

❧ TWENTY-SIX ❧

Two weeks after Dr. Jarom's first visit, Mona stopped scrubbing laundry over the metal washtub when the sound of a motorcycle filled the air. Drying her hands on her apron, she hurried to the front of the house. Alma, Betra, and Alejandro had each left their afternoon chores and gathered near the front door.

The doctor parked the bike in front of them and smiled. He was not alone. "*Iokwe in jibboñ,*" he said, greeting Mona. "*Buenos dias,*" he added for Alejandro's sake.

"*Iokwe in jibboñ,*" Mona and her daughters responded.

"This is Samuel, a Majuro immigration officer," Jarom explained in both Marshallese and Spanish. "He also speaks English and some Spanish. I have come to perform another health checkup on you, and Samuel brings news from your family."

Mona watched Alejandro's face light with excitement. Within seconds Betra was standing at his side, holding fast to his arm.

"Here, sit," Mona said to the group, signaling Alma to help her move two plastic chairs and a crude wooden bench from the side of the house.

Alejandro rushed to help Alma and then sat down next to Betra on the bench, making room for Alma to join them. Mona gestured for Dr. Jarom and Samuel to sit in the chairs, while she stood at the doorway to her home as if protecting it from outsiders.

"What news do you have from my family?"

"They are excited you are alive," Samuel told him with a big smile.

Mona leaned against the doorjamb, crossed her arms in front of her, and listed to Dr. Jarom as he interpreted Samuel's words. She watched Alejandro's face for his reaction. She knew her granddaughter lay in Alejandro's arms at night and had reluctantly given her permission, with Betra's promise to maintain boundaries. Even so, she stayed awake and on alert until she heard Alejandro's snores, glad to know the young man had not disrespected her granddaughter or her home.

But now what? Was he going to leave, abandoning her precious Betra? Or would he send a message back to his family and stay in Namu to marry her granddaughter?

Mona's heart broke into pieces as she watched tears spring to Alejandro's eyes. How could I ever want this young man to stay here a moment longer—away from his mother, who has suffered for so long? But likewise, how can I allow him to take my granddaughter away from me?

"Your phone was water damaged and partially rusted," Samuel said. "We tried for a couple of days to access the contact log and off-load data without success. I finally got the number for your town's mayor's office and left a message. Turns out it was a long holiday weekend, so it took another few days to get a message back from him."

"Did you speak with my mother?" Alejandro asked.

Samuel smiled. "I spoke to her last week. Today was the first ferry out from Majuro to here. I apologize for the long wait."

"How is she?" Alejandro asked.

"She's fine. She screamed, cried, and fainted. Your step-father took the phone while your brother revived her. I held on and waited." Samuel chuckled. "When she came to a few moments later, she asked how you were and then kept saying, *Virgin Santisima!*"

A smile spread across Alejandro's face. "That sounds just like *mi mamá*, thanking the Blessed Virgin Mary. Did she mention my son?"

"Yes. She says she shows him your picture every day he is with her. That he remembers you and wants you home."

The tears that had gathered in Alejandro's eyes fell onto his cheeks. Mona watched the young man's joy. She knew without a doubt she could not ask him to stay, but could she give him her blessing to marry Betra and take her away?

"Are you ready to leave?" Samuel asked. "There's a ferry out this evening. It will take us to Majuro and from there, after some paperwork, we will put you on a plane to Guadalajara. Your brother said he, your mom, sister, and stepfather will meet you at the airport."

"I still need to examine you one last time, Alejandro," Dr. Jarom said. "But I can see from here that you look fit and healthy. You must have gained ten pounds in the last two weeks."

Alejandro looked at Betra and said, "I have been well cared for. Mona, Betra, and Alma are all healers."

Just before walking into the house with the doctor, Alejandro turned to Samuel. "Do I have to leave today?"

Surprised at Alejandro's question, translated by Dr. Jarom, Mona looked at the immigration officer and then back at Alejandro. *Is he going to stay? Is it possible?*

"No, of course, you don't have to leave with us today. There's a ferry out in the morning or one a week from now, although you do need to complete the immigration paperwork I brought with me. But Alejandro, your presence and your story can no longer be kept hidden. Your family said they will let your relatives and friends know you are alive, and the mayor is letting the town know. I expect the news has already gone viral, so reporters will show up here soon. It's only due to the remoteness of this island and the isolation Mona and her daughters have from the other residents in Namu that your presence hasn't already been discovered."

Mona crossed her arms. "I do not want people here, Mr. Samuel. I made that clear from the beginning."

"I know that, ma'am," Dr. Jarom interjected, "and I kept my promise to not reveal Alejandro's story. But Samuel is correct, your privacy is now coming to an end."

Mona noticed tears streaming down Betra's face and moved toward her, taking her into her arms. "You be strong, my little one," she whispered. "God's will be done."

"I don't want him to leave. I love him. He loves me."

Mona and Alma took Betra's arms and walked her away from the house. "Of course you want him to stay," Mona told her granddaughter. "But would you prevent him from seeing his family or holding his son again? You cannot be selfish. You must let him go."

Betra began to sob in her grandmother's arms. "He wants to marry me, Bubu. He said so. He's going to ask your permission to take me with him."

"I imagine he wants to do that. But, Betra, how can I let you go? I am an old woman. I would never see you again. His land is so very far away."

Alma tapped her grandmother on the shoulder. "It would be best if Alejandro leaves with Dr. Jarom and Samuel tonight. On the ferry back to Majuro. If not, our home and our land will be filled with strangers."

Betra pulled away from her grandmother. "No, Bubu. Please. No. Don't make him go. Or let me go with him."

"Don't be foolish, my child. You barely know the boy."

"I can't live without him!" Betra said. Tears streamed down her cheeks. She turned from her grandmother and ran toward Alejandro.

"Betra, please," Mona called after her granddaughter.

Inside the house, Betra ran into Alejandro's arms. "Please stay," she begged. "Doctor Jarom, tell him I love him and want him to stay here."

Dr. Jarom translated what Betra hoped were her words and her heart.

Alejandro's eyes locked with hers and she felt his love pouring back. Stepping away from the doctor, he took her into his arms. "I love you, Betra. I do."

"Then stay. I don't want to live without you," she said. "*Ij iakwe eok.*"

"*Ij iakwe eok,*" Alejandro said, kissing the top of her head.

"Well, you two obviously love each other," Dr. Jarom said with a smile. "You have only two options, Alejandro. Stay here as a couple and confront the media and authorities who will soon be here—or leave together. Right now, or first thing in the morning."

Betra watched Alejandro's face as the doctor translated his options. She saw the pain and knew he was as conflicted as she.

Alejandro felt the weight of Dr. Jarom's words. How could he decide? Looking at Betra he repeated the words she had taught him for I love you. "*Ij iakwe eok.*"

"Maybe there is a third option," he said. "Betra and I go together to Majuro. I meet with the authorities there so Mona's property and home are not invaded by strangers."

Alejandro stopped talking when Mona, Alma, and Samuel walked through the front door. He watched their faces for a reaction as the doctor translated his idea. Not reading a negative or positive reaction, he continued, looking first at Betra and then Alma, "We can get married in Majuro if Mona approves. And then Betra goes with me to Mexico."

He stopped to catch his breath, trying to catch up with the plans flowing through his lips motivated by love. Uncensored by logic.

He caught the look of disapproval from both Mona and Alma and added, "But we will return."

Betra hugged him at the waist and looked up into his eyes. He knew she approved of this option as she repeated, "¡*Sí!* ¡*Sí!*" over and over.

"I do not agree with that option," Mona said.

Alejandro listened to her viewpoint as translated by Jarom, and said, "Please tell her it will not be forever. I promise to return within the year. Just please give me that amount of time to go see my son and family. Then I will return here with Betra...to live."

"How could you return to your life and family and then leave them again? Have you thought about that?" Alma asked.

Alejandro took a deep breath. Alma's question was valid. All eyes were on him as he searched his heart. "I love Betra. I want her to be my wife. My family will meet her, they will see our love and be okay with our return here."

He paused for the doctor to catch up with him. "I will speak with Nando's mother. I will seek permission for joint custody so at times he can visit me here. We can make it work.

"Samuel, what is the distance between Majuro and Guadalajara?"

Samuel responded, "Before our visit today, I researched that. It's a bit over 9,000 kilometers, or nearly 6,000 miles. It is a 35-hour flight, which includes overnight stops."

Alejandro took a seat on his mattress and Betra followed. "Much farther than I thought," he mused, face now in hands. *What do I do?*

He looked up. "Samuel, is it even possible for Betra and I to fly home via the United States? Is that lawful for a Mexican and a Marshallese woman without visas?"

"Your case is special. You would be allowed this one time. I'll have to look into requirements for Betra. But to return here in the future via stops in the United States? I cannot speak to that. And the cost is one thousand U.S. dollars one way per person."

Alejandro looked around the room. "More complicated than I thought," he said. "Mona, would you allow Betra to marry me and travel to Mexico, knowing we may not be able to return for a long time?"

All eyes turned to Mona.

Alejandro waited, holding his breath. In silence, he prayed, "Please Lord, please Lord, let her say yes." His heart burst into both excitement and fear when Mona motioned for Betra and him to approach her.

He stood on her right side. Betra on her left.

They waited.

Mona put her arms around each of them, pulling them close. He could smell the lingering smoke on her clothing from today's lunch of grilled chicken. He could hear ocean waves pounding at high tide outside the doorway. He could see the apprehension in the faces of Alma, Jarom, and Samuel. He could hear the sadness in Mona's voice as she said, "I want to be selfish. I want Betra to stay at my side, to accompany me in my final years."

She looked first at Betra and then Alejandro. "Alejandro, you are the grandson I never had. You have stepped up to care for my small family—fixing our home, working in the garden, fishing to feed us in the very ocean that almost took your life."

Alejandro listened carefully to Mona's words. He continued to pray. Like his mother, he found himself pleading to the *Virgin Santisima*. The thought warmed his heart.

"Your love and bond are admirable," he heard Mona say, followed by the answering of his prayer. "I give you my blessing for whatever choice you make here today."

∾ TWENTY-SEVEN ∾

April 1, 2018
Santa Rosa, California

The alarm startles me out of deep sleep. I take a moment to orient myself to time and place. The brain fog lifts. I'm back home in the States. It's Easter and I need to get ready for Sunday service.

Memories flood in. Another Alejandro dream.

Wait! Was it a dream? My heart is pounding. Is Alejandro alive? He must be. His presence envelopes me. I feel his and Betra's love. My mother's heart understands Mona's dilemma—can she let her granddaughter leave?

I must have fallen asleep last night after hearing the news that Alejandro had been found alive on a remote island.

I throw off the bed covers, pick up my cell phone, and search through Facebook. Nothing there about Alejandro. I check Cesar's and Rosy's pages. Nothing. I'm not sure what that means. Maybe the family hasn't gone public yet?

I click on the La Perlita mayor's page. He announces today's Easter Sunday celebration in the town square. Why hasn't he mentioned Alejandro's miracle reappearance?

Why is his family and the mayor waiting to let the world know?

Was it only a dream?

I don't want to believe that.

Pushed for time, I jump in the shower and prepare for the day—the whole while praying that on this day of miracles, this sacred day when Christians worldwide celebrate Jesus rising from the dead—that my sweet friend Alejandro is alive, somewhere.

And, just maybe, as the La Perlita community—except for Alejandro's family—go about their lives with a fading memory of his disappearance nearly a year ago, this premonition filling me is a sign from above to not give up hope. To never give up hope.

∽

NEVER FORGOTTEN

Originally from Redwood Valley, California, Linda (Cassells) Bello-Ruiz now divides her time in active retirement between Santa Rosa, California, and Barra de Navidad, Jalisco, Mexico.

As a young adult, Ms. Bello-Ruiz founded The House of Hope in San Jose, Costa Rica, a safe-haven for street girls and underage prostitutes. After returning to the United States, she earned a master's degree in psychology from Sonoma State University in Rohnert Park, California.

For twenty-six years, she worked as a bilingual vocational rehabilitation counselor and consulted as a vocational expert on disability in litigation for five of those years. She is the mother of four grown children.

During her months in Mexico, Ms. Bello-Ruiz is active in the town council, spearheads fundraisers in support of schools, is the founder of *Angel Projects*, which helps the less fortunate, and is the co-founder of *Becas por Barra*, a scholarship program that provides financial assistance to selected middle school students so they can attend high school.

Ms. Bello-Ruiz's mantra is, "Lord, how can I be of service? What do You have for me today?"

In her spare time, she writes and teaches writing. Her award-winning first book, *From Tears to Triumph: My Journey to The House of Hope*, and her second book,

Love Thy Neighbor: A Precarious Endeavor, are available on Amazon.

Thank you for reading. If you enjoyed this book, please leave a review on Amazon.

Contact information: email: lmbelloruiz@gmail.com, website: www.lindabelloruiz.com, Facebook page: https://www.facebook.com/LindaBelloRuiz/

⮩ PRAISE FOR
MS. BELLO-RUIZ'S BOOKS ⮨

From Tears to Triumph:
My Journey to The House of Hope

A captivating true story of despair turned into hope. Nineteen-year-old Linda stops on the way home from work to talk to a handsome stranger. That chance meeting on a San Francisco street corner changes the course of her life. Linda's compassionate, gripping, and soul-searching memoir tells the story of her remarkable journey from the dark- 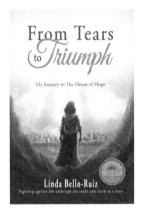 ness of despair and crushed dreams to the creation of a house of hope. Her desperate cry for help brings a spiritual awakening, a two-year life-molding adventure with the controversial Children of God commune, and her decision to leave them. By the age of twenty-two, disillusioned but not defeated, Linda follows a tug on her heart and a voice in her head and moves to Costa Rica where she advocates for street girls and underage prostitutes. Read her story of tears turned to triumph as faith, defiance, and courage propel her forward, fighting against the underage sex trade— one child at a time.

꙰ This is one of the most gripping and inspirational memoirs I have read. It has every quality that makes a page-turner a page-turner—love, loss, betrayal, redemption and renewal, to name a few. I had to remind myself as I read along that this is a true story and not a novel. The thing I love about this woman's story, and what I will keep in my heart always, is her unwavering faith and dedication to God and God's guidance, even in the darkest of times. This memoir is enough to inspire even the most cynical reader—which, I admit, I'm not. —Jo C.

꙰ Thanks to Linda for sharing her amazing story with the world. I found the story well-written and engaging. Her determination and faith were inspiring to me. I knew nothing about the Children of God movement in the 70's and I found her involvement with them extremely interesting, especially the sharp distinction between the activities of the grass-roots members and those of its leadership. It amazed me that someone so young could accomplish as much as she did. I would recommend this book to others. —Rick H.

꙰ Bello-Ruiz's story is compelling and inspirational. Her writing pulls the reader along at every page. I was particularly intrigued by her story of being drawn into the religious cult and how she saw those years. This book has won a number of awards—all well deserved. Bravo! —Cheyenne

꙰ This is an amazing book with a message of hope and courage for everyone. I have read and passed this book on as gifts for all my friends who have had struggles with gaining a productive and meaningful life. She started out in rebellious seeking and gave hope and meaning as a result of her struggling searches. When she was up against negativity and despair, she turned it into a cause for people too beaten down to speak for themselves, and she is still using her voice and experiences to turn hopelessness into a House of Hope. Amazing story and an inspiring woman. —Carolyn Q.

❧ I know from whence this author has come, since I lived in the area in which she was raised and worked in the school district from which she graduated. Her journey from the rural Northern California valley, to San Francisco, to Costa Rica and back is an incredible one. Her story is one that demonstrates faith in God in its purest and most complete form. God provided a "safety net" for her on numerous occasions! To begin this book is to finish it. It is exceedingly well written and holds the reader in its grip throughout. This woman's life has been extraordinary, and she isn't finished yet! God still has work for her to complete. —Carol N.P.

Love Thy Neighbor:
A Precarious Endeavor

In 2010, a young drug lord tied to a prominent Mexican cartel moves next door to an unsuspecting California woman escaping northern winters along the Pacific Coast of Mexico. His lifestyle brings drugs, alcohol and noise into her quiet surroundings. Filled with anger, Rebecca decides to expel him from the neighborhood—requesting assistance from  the local authorities. No assistance arrives. After receiving a prompting to "Love Thy Neighbor," Rebecca faces her fear and sets out to do just that, going against the advice and counsel of friends and family. This gripping story, based on true events, delves into her neighbor's journey from crushed youthful dreams of becoming a professional soccer player to the dire consequences of his life-altering decisions. Follow Rebecca on her own journey from anger to compassion and ultimately an unexpected love for her neighbor, Toro.

> ➢ This was such an incredible story of a path to loving an unlovable person. It seemed such an impossible task. The story weaves its way through the life of a woman pouring her soul into retirement in her paradise (Mexico), to an invasion of that life by a notorious criminal.... Instead of looking for revenge, she starts looking for help from the law and then, incredibly, she sees the man's family and the wonderful children, which changes the course of her revenge to one of love. What a journey and what a spirit. —Carolyn Q.

∾ It is not hard to love the lovable but almost impossible to love the unlovable—except with the help of God. Here the author shares her quest on what it looks like to step out in faith to obey God's command to "Love Thy Neighbor." This was an excellent story that educates the reader on Mexican culture and the situation plaguing so many in Mexico—to wit, the drug cartels. The end made me cry. I thought, "This is how God sees even the evil...why He can love even them." —Michael F.

∾ This story was very insightful. It evokes introspection. Americans usually try to play the victim of the drug trade. Yet Mexico has suffered at a family level with the corrupt seduction of the money, too. Ms. Bello-Ruiz writes a compelling story of a young Mexican boy with high ideals who succumbs to the easy money of selling drugs. What this does to his entire family and the tragedy it brings to a lovely seaside town all lead to the unpredictable ending. The heroine, Rebecca, has a choice to hate or love this neighbor. He lives next door! She chooses to try and salvage the man's soul. How many of us would have taken the chance to love a neighbor like this? Rhetorical question. Read it first, then ask yourself the question. —Quentin G.

∾ Excellent storyteller. The unlikely bond between saint and sinner. I liked the family connections. The story relates how a seemingly well-intentioned young person can follow the wrong path in the fork of the road. A very poignant example of decisions causing intended consequences, especially the deaths of the innocents. —Stan K.

꩜ How we overcome our fears and do what we know is right to do is not always easy—but it is necessary.... This is the kind of book you read and see bits of yourself in, realizing that we all know what it's like to judge others and not allow the example that Jesus Christ set guide us. One of the other things I realized in reading this book is that we have to realize that once we do our part, that is all we can do. We can't make anyone love us and we can't make anyone change. All we can do is share a different way, and sometimes that will lead them to make different decisions. —Cyrus W.

꩜ Love is a decision—and she made that decision. We have been going to Mexico for many years, but as "visitors," you do not see the depth of what is going on due to the drug trade, etc. The author's journey to an understanding of her neighbor is a powerful lesson— she doesn't excuse Toro but comes to grips with what led him to his life. —Carole S.

꩜ The Readers' Favorite Association gives *Love Thy Neighbor* a 5-Star Review:

Based on a real-life story, this is a beautiful story beautifully told. Linda Bello-Ruiz writes with moving simplicity and captures emotions that readers can easily identify with. Her characters are well-developed, and they arrest the attention of readers immediately. This is a story that is as inspiring as it is fast-paced, and features unforgettable characters. From the excellent prose to the deftly written plot, this is every bit an entertaining read. —Ruffina Oserio

❧ I just read *Love thy Neighbor*. It was an awesome read. Thank you, thank you. I try and relate to people what goes on here in this part of Mexico, but this book sooooo puts it all in the right perspective. It is a must read for everyone who comes here. —Jury M.L.

~

Made in the
USA
Monee, IL